Joshua Lax

Historical and Descriptive Poems

Joshua Lax

Historical and Descriptive Poems

ISBN/EAN: 9783744765619

Printed in Europe, USA, Canada, Australia, Japan

Cover: Foto ©Andreas Hilbeck / pixelio.de

More available books at **www.hansebooks.com**

Yours faithfully
Joslina Lax

HISTORICAL

AND

DESCRIPTIVE

POEMS

BY

JOSHUA LAX.

WITH NUMEROUS EXPLANATORY AND OTHER NOTES,

AND

ILLUSTRATED WITH PORTRAITS AND LOCAL VIEWS.

DURHAM: GEO. NEASHAM.
1884.

Dedication.

TO

SAMUEL B. COXON, ESQ.,

IN APPRECIATION OF HIS MANY

ADMIRABLE QUALITIES,

OF HIS

ERUDITION, GOOD TASTE, LOVE OF

BEAUTY, AND ALL THAT IS

TRULY NOBLE AND ELEVATING,

AND OF HIS CONSTANT READINESS TO

RENDER A SERVICE TO THE

GOOD AND DESERVING NEEDY,

THIS WORK IS HUMBLY DEDICATED BY

THE AUTHOR.

Illustrations.

PREFACE.

OVID, in his quaint description of the Temple of
Fame, speaks of the structure as being so designed
as to reproduce, in a subdued form, every word spoken
on sea and shore ; and although, says the poet, the
place was always filled with a confused hubbub of
low dying sounds, many of the voices were spent and
worn before they reached the rendezvous. Whether
the footfalls of the present newcomer will ever echo
in the corridors of the far-famed palace, it would,
perhaps, be premature to conjecture. The writer's
ambition does not soar so high. He has no pretentions
to renown, nor is it without feelings of diffidence that
he ventures to introduce the following pages to the
favour of the public. It has been said that every
man has one or more qualities which may make him
useful both to himself and others ; and if, in the spirit
of this axiom, the perusal of the following pages serves
to heighten the pleasure of the passing hour, and fling
a loftier interest around the ever-flowing stream of
human life, the author seeks no nobler recompense.
Many of the poems are already well known in West

Durham, and if, in their present connected form, they chance to merit a wider circulation, it is to be hoped they will satisfy the expectations of the stranger, not merely in the variety of the subjects chosen, but in purity of tone and sentiment.

The explanatory footnotes attached to some of the longer poems will perhaps recall not a few favourite incidents and half-forgotten legends, which may tend to enhance the interest and usefulness of the work.

My very cordial and sincere thanks are due to the printer and publisher, who has been of untold value to me in the dual capacity of councillor and friend.

JOSHUA LAX.

Shotley Bridge, March, 1884.

List of Subscribers.

———o———

A

Adamson, Mr. Matthew, Burnopfield, 1 copy.
Addison, Mr. J. T., Shotley Bridge, 1 copy.
Ainsworth, Mr. G., Westbank, Consett, 1 copy.
Allendale Cottages, The Working Men's Reading Room, 1 copy.
Allison, Mr., Hamsterley Mill, Lintz Green, 1 copy.
Amos, Mr. Joseph, Shotley Bridge, 1 copy.
Anderson, Mr. James, Black Hedley, Blackhill, 1 copy.
Anderson, Mr. John, woodman, Mosswood, 1 copy.
Annandale, W. M., Esq., Lintz Ford, Lintz Green, 1 copy.
Annandale, James, Esq., J.P., The Briary, Shotley Bridge, 1 copy.
Annandale, Miss, Shotley Grove, Shotley Bridge, 2 copies.
Appleby, Mr. Wm., Leazes, Burnopfield, 1 copy.
Appleton, Mr. John Reed, F.S.A., Western Hill, Durham, 1 copy.
Archbold, Mrs., Sydenham Terrace, Newcastle-on-Tyne, 1 copy.
Arkless, Mr. John, Tantobie, 1 copy.
Armstrong, Mr. Stephen, Holly Lodge, Shotley Bridge, 1 copy.
Armstrong, Mr. Roger, Hamsterley Hall, Lintz Green, 1 copy.
Atkinson, Mr. Robert, Shakespere Terrace, Sunderland, 1 copy.
Atkinson, Mr., Low Hermitage Farm, Satley, Darlington, 1 copy.
Aynsley, Mr. William, Consett, 1 copy.

B

Bainbridge, Mr. T. H., Market Street, Newcastle-on-Tyne, 1 copy.
Bailie, Rev. Alexander, The Manse, Blackhill, 1 copy.
Baitey, Rev. Wm., 4, Sutton Street, Durham, 1 copy.
Bancroft & Fawthorp, Messrs., brush manufacturers, Halifax, Yorks., 2 copies.
Barmby, Rev. James, Vicar of Pittington, Durham, 2 copies.
Barclay, Mr. R. G., Cauldwell, Shotley Bridge, 1 copy.
Barker, Mr. G. C., Derwent Cote, Lintz Green, 1 copy.
Barnes, Chas. E., Esq., Western Hill, Durham, 1 copy.
Barrass, Mr. Alexander, 7, Loadman Street, Scotswood Road, Newcastle-on-Tyne, 1 copy.
Barron, Mr. Cuthbert, Benfieldside Edge Road, Blackhill, 1 copy.
Bates, Mr. J., watchmaker, West Stanley, Chester-le-Street, 1 copy.
Batey, Isaac, Esq., Hexham, 1 copy.
Baynes, Mr. C., Snow's Green, Shotley Bridge, 1 copy.

Beckwith, Rev. J. S., M.A., Walker Vicarage, Newcastle, 1 copy.
Bell, Mr. Joseph, Swiss Cottage, Shotley Bridge, 1 copy.
Bell, Mr. H., Edmondbyers, 1 copy.
Bell, Mr. T., 14, Wood Street, Shotley Bridge, 1 copy.
Bell, Mr. Wilson,'Baybridge, Blanchland, 1 copy.
Belt, Messrs. Geo. & Sons, 23, Groat Market, Newcastle, 1 copy.
Benson, Mr. R. S., Benfieldside Edge Road, Blackhill, 1 copy.
Bennett, Mr. J. R., Northumberland Street, Newcastle, 1 copy.
Bernasconi, Mr. A., 41, Dean Street, Newcastle-on-Tyne, 1 copy.
Best, Mr. F., police constable, Westwood, 1 copy.
Beeley, Mr. Henry, 5, Summer Place, Kidderminster, 1 copy.
Black, Messrs. & Sons, Sea View Works, Berwick, 1 copy.
Blackhill Mechanics' Institute, 1 copy.
Boag, Mr. Hugh, Shotley Hall, Shotley Bridge, 1 copy.
Bolton, W. T., Esq., M.D., Prospect House, Ebchester, 1 copy.
Bolton, Mrs., White House Road, Sunderland, 1 copy.
Bowmaker, Mr. E., 10, Beauclarc Terrace, Sunderland, 1 copy.
Bowey, Mr. John, Castleside, 1 copy.
Booth, John, Esq., Summerdale, Shotley Bridge, 1 copy.
Brady, Mr. Wm., 4, Eltringham Street, Blackhill, 1 copy.
Bramley, Mr. Joseph, Ebchester, 1 copy.
Brears, Mr. W., Redwell Hills, Leadgate, 1 copy.
Brewis, Mr. Wm., Newlands Grange, Blackhill, 1 copy.
Britton, Mr. Geo., Friargate, New Scarborough, Wakefield, 1 copy.
Brotherhood, Mr. W., Lanchester, 1 copy.
Brodie, Mr. John, Front Street, Shotley Bridge, 1 copy.
Brodie, Mr. Adam, Town Hall, Consett, 1 copy.
Brooks, John C., Esq., 14, Lovaine Place, Newcastle, 1 copy.
Brooks, Miss, Workhouse, Lanchester, 1 copy.
Brown, Mr. N., Front Street, Shotley Bridge, 1 copy.
Brown, Mr. Thomas, Front Street, Shotley Bridge, 1 copy.
Brown, Mr. Wm., mason, Shotley Bridge, 1 copy.
Brown, Mr. Geo., Wood Street, Shotley Bridge, 1 copy.
Brown, Mr. Joseph, 6, Rose Mount, Consett, 1 copy.
Brown, Mr. Peter, Shotley Bridge, 1 copy.
Brown, Mr. Ralph, Baxton Burn, Blackhill, 1 copy.
Brown, Mr. Jno., Little Black Hedley, Blackhill, 1 copy.
Brown, Mrs. D. A., Pittington, Durham, 1 copy.
Bruce, Mr. Thomas, Green Street, Shotley Bridge, 1 copy.
Bruce, Mr. Thos., 3, Green Street, Shotley Bridge, 1 copy.
Bryson, Rev. D., Shadforth, Durham, 1 copy.
Buckham, Mr. John, Lanchester, 1 copy.
Buckham, Mr. George, Lanchester, 1 copy.
Bullock, Mr. Jno., gardener, Snow's Green, Shotley Bridge, 1 copy.

Bulman, Mr. Thomos, Birkhott, Muggleswick, 1 copy.
Burdess, Mr. Thos., 31, Thomas Street, Monkwearmouth, 1 copy.
Burdess, Mr. Ed., Dock Street East, Monkwearmouth, 1 copy.
Burton, Mr. Eli, Poplar House, Shotley Bridge, 1 copy.
Bushby, Mr. Matthew, Blackhall Mill, Lintz Green, 1 copy.
Byers, Mr. H. (Nicholson & Co.), Pilgrim Street, Newcastle, 2 copies.

C

Cain, J. C., Esq., Woodbine Villa, Gateshead, 1 copy.
Carr, J. Rodham, Esq., LL.D., Carr Stones, Wolsingham, 1 copy.
Calvert, Mr. John, Sherburn House, Consett, 1 copy.
Campbell, Mr. J. W., Fawcett Street, Sunderland, 1 copy.
Campbell, Rev. Edward, Shotley Bridge, 1 copy.
Campbell, Mr. W., Jun., 16, Blandford Street, Sunderland, 1 copy.
Campbell, Mr. W., Front Street, Shotley Bridge, 1 copy.
Campbell, Rev. A., Front Street, Shotley Bridge, 1 copy.
Carr, M., Esq., Ebchester Hall, Ebchester, 2 copies.
Carr, Mr. Jas. D., Sunniside, Tow Law, 1 copy.
Carruthers, Mr. John, Castleside, 1 copy.
Cawthorne, Mr. Ed. P., butcher, Shotley Bridge, 1 copy.
Chapman, Miss Emma, Shotley House, Shotley Bridge, 1 copy.
Charlton, Mr. William, Burnopfield, 1 copy.
Charlton, Mr. Thos., timber merchant, Burnopfield, 1 copy.
Charlton, Mr. W., Dene House, Ebchester, 1 copy.
Charlton, Mr. Thos., Snow's Green Road, Shotley Bridge, 1 copy.
Charlton, Mr. John, High Waskerley, Shotley Bridge, 1 copy.
Chaytor, Mr. R., Hamsterley Colliery, Ebchester, 1 copy.
Cheesman, Mr. W., Iveston, 1 copy.
Cherry, Miss, Crossgate, Durham, 1 copy.
Cheyne, Mr. James, Shotley Bridge, 1 copy.
Chisholm, Mr. J., engineer, North Skelton Mines, Saltburn, 1 copy.
Christopher, Mrs., North-Eastern Hotel, Blackhill, 1 copy.
Christopher, Mr. John, Durham Road, Blackhill, 1 copy.
Cochrane, Brodie, Esq., Aldin Grange, 1 copy.
Cockin, Rev. W., M.A., Vicar of Medomsley, 2 copies.
Clark, Robert, Esq., Lintz Green House, Lintz Green, 1 copy.
Close, Mr. John, Medomsley, 1 copy.
Collinson, Mr. John, Grove Schools, Shotley Bridge, 1 copy.
Collinson, Mr. John, Consett, 1 copy.
Collinson, Mr. George W., Salem Street P.O., Sunderland, 1 copy.
Coulson, Mr. T., Benfieldside Edge Road, Blackhill, 1 copy.
Coulson, Mr. Thomas, Birtley, Chester-le-Street, 1 copy.
Coulson, Mr. Joseph, Front Street, Shotley Bridge, 1 copy.
Cook, Mr. John G., 9, Cort Street, Blackhill, 1 copy.

Cook, Mr. John, 3, Ledger Terrace, Blackhill, 1 copy.
Coupland, Mr. M., Westwood House, Ebchester, 1 copy.
Cowen, Jos., Esq., M.P., 23, Onslow Square, London, S.W., 1 copy.
Coxon, S. B., Esq., 7, Westminster Chambers, Victoria Street, Westminster, London, 12 copies.
Coxon, Mr. Ed., Cutlers' Hall Road, Blackhill, 1 copy.
Cranston, Mr. R., Shotley Bridge, 1 copy.
Crow, A. T., Jun., Esq., Belle Vue Park, Sunderland, 1 copy.
Cruickshank, Mr. Alexander, 22, Union Street, Wallsend, 1 copy.
Cumming, Mr. John, Langley West House, Langley Park, 1 copy.
Currie & Hutchinson, Messrs., chemists, Side, Newcastle, 1 copy.
Curry, Mr. J. T., Delves Lane, Consett, 1 copy.
Curtis & Harvey, Messrs., 74, Lombard St., London, E.C., 1 copy.
Cuthbertson, Rev. James, 2, Esk Terrace, Whitby, 1 copy.

D

Davey, Mr. Wm., Snow's Green, Shotley Bridge, 1 copy.
Davison, Mr. J. W., ironmonger, Consett, 1 copy.
Davison, Mr. Charles, Front Street, Consett, 1 copy.
De Pledge, Rev. J. P., M.A., Satley, 1 copy.
Dickinson, Robert, Esq., J.P., Shotley House, Shotley Bridge, 1 copy.
Dickinson, Mrs., Belle Vue House, Shotley Bridge, 2 copies.
Dickinson, Mrs. W. R., Priestfield Lodge, Lintz Green, 1 copy.
Dickinson, William, Esq., The Villa, Shotley Bridge, 1 copy.
Dixon, Mr. John, Benfieldside Edge Road, Blackhill, 1 copy.
Dixon, Mr. Robert, Shotley Estate, Shotley Bridge, 1 copy.
Dixon, Mr. Robert, Broad Oak, Ebchester, 1 copy.
Dixon, Mr. Edward, Ebchester Mill, Ebchester, 1 copy.
Dixon, Mr. Jos., 15, Barrington Terrace, Hetton-le-Hole, Fence Houses, 1 copy.
Dixon, Mr. Andrew, Apperley, Stocksfield, 1 copy.
Dixon, Mr. William, The Lodge, Lanchester, 1 copy.
Dixon, Mr. John, Littletown Farm, Durham, 1 copy.
Dobson, Mr. Henry, The Briary, Shotley Bridge, 1 copy.
Dodd, Mr. H., Rokeby Villa, Durham, 1 copy.
Douglas, Mr. James, Co-operative Store, Shotley Bridge, 1 copy.
Douglas, Chas. D. & Co., 15, Queenhithe, Upper Thames Street, London, 1 copy.
Douglass, Rev. Wm., Hawthorn Cottage, Shotley Bridge, 1 copy.
Dowson, Mr. Jacob, Blackhill, 1 copy.
Duncan, Mr. Wm., editor *Durham Chronicle*, 1 copy.
Dunn, Mr. Thomas, Lanchester, 1 copy.

Drummond, Mr. John, Hole House, Blackhill, 1 copy.
Drummond, Mr. John, Kiln Pit Hill, Riding Mill, 1 copy.

E

East, J. G., Esq., Dunster House, Durham, 1 copy.
Eden, Mr. Geo., merchant tailor, West Street, Gateshead, 1 copy.
Egdell, Mr. J. J., 116, Northumberland Street, Newcastle-on-Tyne, 1 copy.
Eltringham, Mr. Joseph, Benfieldside, 2 copies.
Eltringham, Mr. W., Highgate, Blackhill, 1 copy.
Eltringham, Mr. G., Blackhill, 1 copy.
Elliott, Rev. T., Blackhill, 1 copy.
Elliott, Mr. William, assistant overseer, Consett, 2 copies.
Elliott, Mr. Jos. F., St. Ives' Road, Leadgate, 1 copy.
Elsdon, Mr. M., Ebchester, 1 copy.
England, Mr. John B., Derwent Cote Farm, 1 copy.
Erskine, Mr. Geo. H., 15, Adelaide Terrace, New Benwell, Newcastle-on-Tyne, 1 copy.

F

Fairley, Jas., Esq., Craghead, Chester-le-Street, 2 copies.
Fairlamb, Mr. J. O., Cutlers' Hall, Blackhill, 1 copy.
Fairlamb, Mr. John, 7, Cutlers' Hall Road, Blackhill, 1 copy.
Fairlamb, Mr. Thomas, 8, Cutlers' Hall Road, Blackhill, 1 copy.
Farrar, Rev. Wesley, M.A., The Vicarage, Castleside, 1 copy.
Farrar, Rev. H. W., Chaplain Tyne Mission Ship, South Shields, 1 copy.
Fawcett, Mr. John, 100, Tynemouth Road, Heaton, Newcastle, 1 copy.
Featherstonehaugh, Rev. W., M.A., Edmondbyers, 1 copy.
Pewster, Mr. Anthony, Newlands, Ebchester, 1 copy.
Finlayson, Bousfield & Co., Messrs., thread manufacturers, Johnstone, Renfrewshire, 2 copies.
Fitzpatrick, Mr. S. J., Bridge Hill, 1 copy.
Fleming, P. R. & Co., 29, Argyle Street, Glasgow, 1 copy.
Forster, Miss E. A., Shotley Bridge, 1 copy.
Forster, Mr. John, builder, Medomsley, 1 copy.
Forster, Mr. J. W., Shotley Bridge, 1 copy.
Forster, Mr. George, police-constable, Shotley Bridge, 1 copy.
Fowler, James, Esq., Mayor of Durham, 1 copy.
Frankland, Mr. Rd., 4, Cross Derwent Street, Blackhill, 1 copy.
Frankland, Mr. Michael, Derwent Street, Blackhill, 1 copy.

French, Mr. W., Fore Street, Hexham, 1 copy.

G

Galloway, Mr. W., Bensham Tower, Gateshead, 2 copies.
Gibson, Mr. Michael, Edge Road, Benfieldside, 1 copy.
Gilchrist, Mr. James, Longfield House, Marley Hill, 1 copy.
Gilmour, John, Esq., Llwynypia, near Pontypridd, So. Wales, 1 copy.
Gledstone, Mr. T. L., North-Eastern Bank, Consett, 1 copy.
Gledstone, Rev. J. P., 63, Upper Tulse Hill, London, S.W., 1 copy.
Gledstone, Mr. John, Blackwell, Darlington, 1 copy.
Golightly, Elizabeth, Springfield, Shotley Bridge, 1 copy.
Gourley, Rev. G. M., Vicar of Blanchland, 1 copy.
Green, Mr. William, Mare Burn Cottage, Blackhill, 1 copy.
Green, Mrs., grocer, Lanchester, 1 copy.
Greenwell, Rev. Wm., M.A., D.C.L., F.S.A., Durham, 1 copy.
Gregson, W., Esq., Baldersby, Thirsk, 1 copy.
Gribbens, Mr. John, Greenwood, Shotley Bridge, 1 copy.
Ground, Mr. Wm., Derwent House, Shotley Bridge, 1 copy.
Guthrie, Mr. John, Shotley Grove, Shotley Bridge, 1 copy.

H

Hall, Mr. Ralph, Shotley Bridge, 1 copy.
Hall, Mr. Jesse, Market Street, Consett, 2 copies.
Hall, Mr. Robert, Baxton Burn, Shotley Bridge, 1 copy.
Hallatt, Mr. C., 206, Bradford Street, Birmingham, 1 copy.
Handcock, Mr., Barcus Close, Lintz Green, 1 copy.
Harker, Mr., Consett Station, 1 copy.
Hardy, Miss, Front Street, Shotley Bridge, 1 copy.
Harris, Mr. Daniel, draper, Spen, Lintz Green, 1 copy.
Harrison, Mr. George, Front Street, Shotley Bridge, 1 copy.
Harrison, Mr. Thomas, Front Street, Shotley Bridge, 1 copy.
Harrison, Mr. J., Sherburn Colliery Station, Durham, 1 copy.
Hawdon, Mr. George, Consett, 1 copy.
Hedley, Geo., Esq., J.P., Burnhopeside Hall, Lanchester, 1 copy.
Hedley, W. H., Esq., Manor House, Medomsley, 1 copy.
Henderson, Mr. Richard, Ebchester, 1 copy.
Heppell, Mr. Wm., Espershiels, Riding Mill, 1 copy.
Heymer, Mr. John, Benfieldside, 4 copies.
Hobson, Mr. George, Harperley Mills, Lintz Green, 1 copy.
Hodges, Mr. Charles C., Hexham, 1 copy.
Hodgson, Mr. Thomas, draper, Blackhill, 3 copies.
Hodgson, J. W., Esq., Bradley Lodge, Dipton, 1 copy.

Hogg, Mr. W., 42, Westwood, 1 copy.
Hooppell, Rev. R. E., M.A., LL.D., Byers Green Rectory, 1 copy.
Hopper, Dr., Dempsterville, Felling-on-Tyne, 1 copy.
Hopper, Mr. Robert, *Chronicle* Office, Durham, 1 copy.
Houliston, Mr. A., Shotley Bridge, 1 copy.
Howie, Mr. W. J., 53, Derwent Street, Blackhill, 1 copy.
Howie, Mr. Thomas, Waterworks, West Hartlepool, 1 copy.
Hudspith, Mr. Dickson, Carterway Head, Blackhill, 1 copy.
Hull, Mr. Matthew, 9, Cutlers' Hall, Blackhill, 1 copy.
Humble, Mr., Newcastle-on-Tyne, 1 copy.
Hunt, Mr. George, Shotley House, Shotley Bridge, 1 copy.
Hunter, Miss, Derwent Villa, Shotley Bridge, 1 copy.
Hunter, Mr. E. H., Derwent House, Seaham Harbour, 1 copy.
Hunter, Miss, Haswell Lane, Fence Houses, 1 copy.
Hunter, Mr. John G., Littletown Farm, Durham, 1 copy.
Huntley, Mr. Joseph, 24, Derby Street, Sunderland, 1 copy.
Hutchinson, Mr. T., Blanchland, 1 copy.
Hyden, Mr. G. T., Sherburn Terrace, Consett, 1 copy.

J

Imrie, Mr. David, 1, Tin Mill Place, Blackhill, 1 copy.
Ingles, Mr. James, 146, Manchester Road, Warrington, 1 copy.
Irving, Mr. Thomas, Westwood Farm, Ebchester, 1 copy.

J

Jackson, Mr. Robert, *Guardian* Office, Consett, 1 copy.
James, Walter H., Esq., M.P., 6, Whitehall Gardens, London, 1
copy.
Jamieson, Mrs., Durham Road, Blackhill, 1 copy.
Jenkins, W., Esq., J.P., Consett Hall, Consett, 4 copies.
Jenkins, Rev. E. W., Carey Cottage, Blackhill, 2 copies.
Jewers, Mr. John, Benfieldside Edge Road, Shotley Bridge, 1 copy.
Jewitt, Mr. Robson, Castleside, 1 copy.
Johnson, Mr. Ed., 26, Wood Street, Shotley Bridge, 1 copy.
Johnson, Mr. Wm., Unthank, Kiln Pit Hill, Riding Mill, 1 copy.
Johnson, Mr. Geo., Benfieldside Edge Road, Blackhill, 1 copy.
Johnstone, Mr. Thomas, 24, Cort Street, Blackhill, 1 copy.
Jones, Dr., Court House, Toypany, Glamorganshire, 1 copy.

K

Kirsopp, Mr. John, Shotley Bridge, 1 copy.

Kitching Bros., Messrs., Kingston Brush Works, Hull, 1 copy.
Kidd, Mr. John, 6, Mount Pleasant, Consett, 2 copies.
Kyle, Mr. Robert, Crookgate, Burnopfield, 1 copy.
Kirkup, Mr. John, Consett Station, 1 copy.
Kearney, Rev. Canon, The Brooms, Leadgate, 1 copy.
Keenleyside, Mr., Crook Hall, Consett, 1 copy.
Kane, Mr. J. J., 2, Princess Street, Gateshead, 1 copy.
Kirkup, Mr. J. S., Stanifordam, Blackhill, 1 copy.

L

Laidlaw, Messrs. R. and Sons, Manor Chare, Newcastle-on-Tyne, 1 copy.
Lamb, Mr. Henry, Ledger Terrace, Blackhill, 1 copy.
Lamb, Mr. Richard, Belle Vue, Shotley Bridge, 1 copy.
Lammonby, Mr. Thomas, Leadgate, 1 copy.
Latimer, Richard, Esq., Whitley, Newcastle-on-Tyne, 2 copies.
Latimer, Rev. A., Loftus-in-Cleveland, Yorkshire, 1 copy.
Laws, Messrs. J. & Co., Rae Street, Glasgow, 1 copy.
Lax, Mr. William, Llwynypia House, Pontypridd, Glamorganshire, 1 copy.
Lax, Mr. Prosser, Jacksonville, Illinois, U.S.A., 1 copy.
Lax, Miss V. V., Jacksonville, Illinois, U.S.A., 1 copy.
Lax, Mr. Edward C., Jacksonville, Illinois, U.S.A., 2 copies.
Lax, Mr. Newark, Jacksonville, Illinois, U.S.A., 1 copy.
Lazenby, Mr. J. B., Shotley Bridge, 1 copy.
Leadbitter, Mr. James, 22, Cutlers' Hall, Blackhill, 1 copy.
Le Keux, Mrs., Old Elvet, Durham, 1 copy.
Leslie, Mr. John, Post Office, Shotley Bridge, 1 copy.
Leslie, Mr. Surtees, 99, Mantua Street, Falcon Lane, Battersea, London, S.W., 1 copy.
Leslie, Mr. Urwin, Post Office, Shotley Bridge, 1 copy.
Leslie, Miss, Post Office, Shotley Bridge, 1 copy.
Leybourne, Miss Lizzie, Margery Flatts, Lanchester, 1 copy.
Leybourne, Mr. S., Derwent Hill, 1 copy.
Leybourne, Mr. S., Jun., Front Street, Shotley Bridge, 1 copy.
Leybourne, Mrs. Geo., Castleside, 1 copy.
Lilburn, Chas., Esq., Glenside, Sunderland, 1 copy.
Lisle, Mr. John, Front Street, Shotley Bridge, 1 copy.
Lisle, Mr. Ralph, Wood Street, Shotley Bridge, 1 copy.
Littlefair, Mr. William, Lanchester, 1 copy.
Locke, Blackett & Co., Messrs., Newcastle-on-Tyne, 1 copy.
Lockhart, Louis C., Esq., Hexham, 1 copy.
Lockwood, Mr. Joseph, Spital Hill, Sheffield, 1 copy.

Logan, William, Esq., Stobbilee House, Langley Park, Durham, 1 copy.
Longstaff, Miss, Pierremont Crescent, Darlington, 1 copy.
Longstaffe, Mr. S. F., F.R.H.S., Norton, 1 copy.
Lough, Mrs., 42, Harewood Square, London, N.W.
Lough, Mr. Wm., blacksmith, Consett, 1 copy.
Lowery, Mr. Robert, High Pittington, Durham, 1 copy.
Lowery, Mr. R. A., High Pittington, Durham, 1 copy.
Lovett, Mr. James, Blackhill, 1 copy.
Lucas, Mrs., Amberley Street, Sunderland, 5 copies.
Lumsden, Mr. J. P., Lockerbie, Dumfriesshire, 1 copy.

M

Macdonald, Mr. John, Cutlers' Hall, Blackhill, 1 copy.
Mackey, Mr. W., Benfieldside, 1 copy.
Mackey, Mr. Thomas, Benfieldside, 1 copy.
Mackey, Mr. John, Highgate, Blackhill, 1 copy.
Maclauchlan, Mr. Hugh S., 14, Buckingham Street, Adelphi, London, W.C., 1 copy.
Makepeace, Mr. J. N., Institute Terrace, Crook, 1 copy.
Marley, T. E. F., Esq., Fell Mount, Ulverston, 1 copy.
Marshall, Mr. Robert, Highgate, Blackhill, 1 copy.
Marston, Mr. H. C., Ross's Hotel, Edinbrough, 3 copies.
Mason, Mr. George, 19, Foundry Road, Blackhill, 1 copy.
Maxwell, J. A. H., Shotley Bridge Station, 1 copy.
McColvin, Mr. Colin Campbell, Newmarket Street, Consett, 1 copy
McIntosh, Mr. Duncan, Snow's Green, Shotley Bridge, 1 copy.
McKeeth, Mr. John, Villiers Street, Sunderland, 1 copy.
McKeeth, Mr. J. F., Villiers Street, Sunderland, 2 copies.
McLauchlin, Miss, Lanchester, 1 copy.
McPherson, Mr. Allan, grocer, Tantobie, 1 copy.
Meadows, Miss Susan, Shotley House, Shotley Bridge, 1 copy.
Menham, Mr. Michael, Hendon Old Station, Sunderland, 1 copy.
Metcalf, Mr. W., Broxbourne Terrace, Sunderland, 1 copy.
Metcalf, Mr. Henry, Fawcett Street, Sunderland, 1 copy.
Mewes, Mr. John, Jun., 21, Durham Road, Blackhill, 1 copy.
Milburn, Mr. John, Belford, Northumberland, 1 copy.
Mitchinson, Robert, Esq., Catchgate House, 1 copy.
Moffatt, Mr. J. S., Shotley Bridge, 1 copy.
Mole, Mr. Anthony, 94, Park Road, Newcastle-on-Tyne, 1 copy.
Mold, Miss S., Shotley House, Shotley Bridge, 1 copy.
Monks, Col., Aden Cottage, Durham, 1 copy.
Moody, Mr. B., Ebchester, 1 copy.

Moody, Mr. George, Ebchester, 1 copy.
Moon, Mr. John, Cemetery Road, Blackhill, 1 copy.
Moore, Mr. Wm. John, 29, Wood Street, Shotley Bridge, 1 copy.
Moore, Mr. William, Ashfield, Shotley Bridge, 1 copy.
Moore, Mr. William, Bridge End, Shotley Bridge, 1 copy.
Morgan, Mr. Nicholas, 7, Salem Hill, Snnderland, 1 copy.
Mosley, Mr. Charles, Shotley Bridge, 1 copy.
Muir, Mr. John Taylor, 20, Bessemer Street, Blackhill, 1 copy.
Muir, Rev. Joseph, Benfieldside Edge Road, Blackhill, 1 copy.
Mullen, Mr. John, Pilgrim Street, Newcastle-on-Tyne, 1 copy.
Murray, D. W., Esq., Jesmond Park, Newcastle-on-Tyne, 1 copy.
Murray, Mr. Richard, Benfieldside House, Blackhill, 1 copy.
Murray, Mr. J. S., Umguni House, Blackhill, 1 copy.
Murray, Mr. John G., Shotley Bridge, 1 copy.
Muse, Mr. J. T., Castleside House, 1 copy.

N

Neasham, Mr., Middlesbro', 1 copy.
Neilson, Mr. John S., 10, Egerton Street, Sunderland, 1 copy.
Nelson, Mr. Wm., 74, Arundel Street, Sheffield, 2 copies.
Nicholson, Mr. C. W., Baxton Burn, Blackhill, 1 copy.
Nicholson, Mr. F. C., 46, Dunn Street, Newcastle, 1 copy.
Nicholson, Mr. George, Leadgate, 1 copy.
Nicholson, Mr. John, Otterburn Terrace, Newcastle, 4 copies.
Nixon, Mr. Thomas, joiner, Edge Road, Benfieldside, 1 copy.
Noble, Mr. Mark, Consett Station, 1 copy.
North of England School Furnishing Co., Darlington, 3 copies.
Nuttall, Rev. J. K., 13, The Oaks, Sunderland, 1 copy.

O

Oley, Mr. Joseph, Wood Street, Shotley Bridge, 4 copies.
Oley, Mr. Christopher, Cutlers' Hall Road, Blackhill, 1 copy.
Oley, Mrs. H., Whittonstall, 2 copies.
Oliver, Mr. Robt., Shotley Field Mill, 1 copy.
Oliver, Mr. John, grocer, Stanley, 3 copies.
Ormerod, Mr. D., Shotley Bridge, 1 copy.
Osborne, Mr. John, Shotley Bridge, 1 copy.
Osborne, Mr. Pattinson, Blackhill, 1 copy.

P

Palliser, Mr. James, Foundry Row, Blackhill, 1 oopy.

Park, Mr. Robert, Mount Pleasant, Consett, 1 copy.
Parkinson, Mr. G., Sherburn, Durham, 2 copies.
Parkinson, Mr. Henry, Railway Terrace, Fence Houses, 2 copies.
Parkinson, Mr. John L., Sherburn, Durham, 1 copy.
Parkinson, Mr. Geo., Jun., Sherburn, Durham, 1 copy.
Parnaby, Mr. Chris., Cemetery Road, Blackhill, 1 copy.
Patterson, Mr. Edward, Shotley Bridge, 2 copies.
Patterson, Mr. George, Benfieldside Edge Road, 1 copy.
Pattinson, Mr. Thomas, Castleside, 1 copy.
Pattinson, Mr. Wm., Castleside, 1 copy.
Pearson, Mr. Henry, Edge Road, Benfieldside, 1 copy.
Pearson, Mr. Geo., Airyholme, Kilnpit Hill, Riding Mill, 1 copy.
Pease, Sir Jos. W., Bart., M.P., Hutton Hall, Gisborough, 1 copy.
Peile, Geo., Esq., Greenwood, Shotley Bridge, 1 copy.
Pescod, Mr. John, Neville Street, Durham, 1 copy.
Petherick, Mr. John, Blackhill, 1 copy.
Pickering, Mr. John, Acton, Blanchland, 1 copy.
Powell, Mr. Thomas, Belmont, Durham, 1 copy.
Powell, Mr. M., 4, Union Place, Gateshead, 1 copy.
Priestman, Jon., Esq., Derwent Lodge, Shotley Bridge, 4 copies.
Priestman, F., Esq., Holly Lodge, Shotley Bridge, 1 copy.
Pringle, Thos., Esq., Tanfield Lea, 2 copies.
Proud, Mr. John, newsagent, Durham Road, Blackhill, 1 copy.
Proudlock, Mr. R. E., 7, Broadwell Row, Oldbury, Birmingham,
    1 copy.
Proudlock, Mr. William, St. Neots, Huntingdonshire, 1 copy.
Purvis, Mr. Ralph, Edge Road, Benfieldside, 1 copy.

Q

Quin, Mr. Stephen, Westgate Road, Newcastle, 1 copy.

R

Raine, Rev. F., Hexham, 1 copy.
Radcliffe, James, Esq., Stafford Villa, South Stockton, 1 copy.
Ramsay, Mr. Wm., Baxton Burn, Blackhill, 1 copy.
Reed, Mr. W., Old Surgery, Blackhill, 1 copy.
Reed, Mr. Gawen, Consett Station, Blackhill, 1 copy.
Reed, R. B., Esq., Springfield, Forest Hall, Newcastle, 1 copy.
Reed, Robt., Esq., Lintz Colliery, Lintz Green, 1 copy.
Reid, Mr. Geo., grocer, Blackhill, 1 copy.
Renton, W. M., Esq., M.D., Orchard House, Shotley Bridge, 4
    copies.

Renton, Geo., Esq., M.D., Viewlands, Blackhill, 2 copies.
Rewcastle, Cuthbert, Esq., Hodgkin, Barnett & Company's Bank, Newcastle, 1 copy.
Richardson, Mr. Geo., Shotley Bridge, 2 copies.
Richardson, Mr. John J., Shotley Bridge, 1 copy.
Richardson, Mrs., Springfield, Shotley Bridge, 1 copy.
Richardson, Mr. Robert, Newbottle, Fence Houses, 1 copy.
Richardson, Mr. Wm., 6, Allendale Cottages, 1 copy.
Richardson, Mr. Geo., West View House, Shotley Bridge, 1 copy.
Richardson, Alderman T. R., Durham, 1 copy.
Richardson, Chas., Esq., Shotley Bridge, 1 copy.
Richley, Mr. M., Durham Road, Blackhill, 2 copies.
Ridley, Mr. G., Shotley Bridge, 1 copy.
Ridley, Mr. Matthew, Snow's Green, Shotley Bridge, 1 copy.
Rimington, Mr. J. M., Whitley, Northumberland, 1 copy.
Rippon, Mr. Robert, Wood Street, Shotley Bridge, 1 copy.
Ritson, Mr. W. H., Lanchester, 1 copy.
Ritson, Wm., Esq., Woodley Field, Hexham, 2 copies.
Ritson, U. A., Esq., J.P., 18, Hawthorn Terrace, Newcastle, 1 copy.
Roberts, Messrs. W. & Co., 4, Summer Row, Birmingham, 2 copies.
Robinson, Thos. W. U., Esq., F.S.A., Hatfield House, Houghton-le-Spring, 2 copies.
Robinson, J. Hastings, Esq., Church Stretton, Shropshire, 1 copy.
Robinson, Mr. W., grocer, Medomsley, 1 copy.
Robinson, Mr. Thomas, Allansford, Blackhill, 1 copy.
Robinson, Mr. Geo. T., Derwent Street, Blackhill, 1 copy.
Robinson, Mr. Wm. Durham Road, Blackhill, 1 copy.
Robinson, Mr. Thomas, joiner, Medomsley, 1 copy.
Robinson, Mr. F., 15, Allendale Cottages, 1 copy.
Robinson, Mr. Robt., Pittington, Durham, 1 copy.
Robinson, Miss, Front Street, Shotley Bridge, 1 copy.
Robson, Mr. Geo., Edmondbyers, 1 copy.
Robson, Mr. Geo., miller, Shotley Bridge, 1 copy.
Robson, Mr. W., 5, Wesley Terrace, Dipton, 1 copy.
Robson, Mr. John, grocer's assistant, Spa Well Cottage, Shotley Bridge, 1 copy.
Robson, Mr. John, cartwright, Whittonstall, Stocksfield, 1 copy.
Robson, Mr. Robt., merchant, Castleside, 1 copy.
Roddam, Mr. J., Broad Chare, Newcastle, 1 copy.
Ross-Lewin, Rev. G. H., M.A., Vicarage, Benfieldside, 2 copies.
Ross-Lewin, Rev. H. H., Vicarage, Benfieldside, 1 copy.
Rounthwaite, Mr. J. W., surveyor, Blackhill, 1 copy.
Rutherford, Mr. Thomas, 218, High Street, Sunderland, 1 copy.
Rutland, Mr. Geo., Bank, Shotley Bridge, 1 copy.

S

Salkeld, Mr. R. W., manager *Durham Advertiser*, 1 copy.
Seed, Mr. John, Temperance Hall, Shotley Bridge, 1 copy.
Schellenberg, Mr., Consett, 1 copy.
Scott, Mr. W. J., Sycamores, Castleside, 1 copy.
Scott, Mr. J., East Parade, Consett, 1 copy.
Scott, Mr. James, Blaydon Saw Mills, Blaydon-on-Tyne, 1 copy.
Shaw, Mr. R. W., Villa Real, Leadgate, 1 copy.
Shell, Mr. Wm., Barr House, Consett, 1 copy.
Shell, Mr. Wm., Jun., Consett Station, Benfieldside, 1 copy.
Sherlock, Mr. Robt., Gold Hill, Waskerley, Darlington, 1 copy.
Sherritt, Mr. John, Cutlers' Hall Road, Shotley Bridge, 1 copy.
Shimmin, Mr. Geo., 36, Fawcett Street, Sunderland, 1 copy.
Shotton, Mr., Blackhill, 1 copy.
Shotton, Miss, Randolph Street, Sunderland, 1 copy.
Siddell, Thomas, Esq., Viewfield, Blackhill, 1 copy.
Siddle, Mr. Geo., Front Street, Shotley Bridge, 1 copy.
Siddle, Mr. N. C., Watling Villa, Willington, Durham, 1 copy.
Simpson, Mr. Ralph, 172, Prince Consort Road, Gateshead, 1 copy.
Slack, Mr. John, bookseller, North Road, Durham, 1 copy.
Sloane, Mr. Ed., postmaster, Blackhill, 1 copy.
Smith, Geo. G. Taylor, Esq., J.P., Broadwood Park, 1 copy.
Smith, Thos. Taylor, Esq., Greencroft Park, 1 copy.
Smith, Mrs., 23, Woodbine Street, Sunderland, 1 copy.
Smith, Rev. H., Wesleyan minister, Bedale, Yorks., 1 copy.
.Smith, Mr. Richd., Benfieldside, 1 copy.
Smith, Mr. John, Rose Cottage, Shotley Bridge, 1 copy.
Smith, Mr. John, East House, Medomsley, 1 copy.
Smith, Mr. Thomas, ironfounder, Blaydon-on-Tyne, 1 copy.
Smith, Mr. John G., Coppice Hall, near Bilston, 1 copy.
Smith, Mr. J. G., The Hencotes, Hexham, 1 copy.
Smith, Mr. Francis, *Chronicle* Office, Durham, 1 copy.
Smith, Mr. Geo., 11, Queen Street, Consett, 1 copy.
Smith, Mr. John, The Grange, Castleside, 1 copy.
Soulsby, Mr. Joseph, Philadelphia, Fence Houses, 1 copy.
Spraggon, Miss, Wood Street, Shotley Bridge, 1 copy.
Spraggon, Mr. John, Shotley Bridge, 1 copy.
Stephenson, Mr. Charles, Cemetery Road, Blackhill, 1 copy.
Stoddart, Mr. Wm., Ebchester, 1 copy.
Stout, Mr. Abraham, *Advertiser* Office, Durham, 1 copy.
Strachan, Mr. Wm., Blackhill, 1 copy.
Summerson, Mr. Michael, 14, Vane Terrace, Seaham Harbour,
    1 copy.

Surtees, Miss, Hamsterley Hall, Lintz Green, 1 copy.
Surtees, Miss Eleanor, Hamsterley Hall, 1 copy.
Surtees, Mr. H., Edmondbyers, 1 copy.
Surtees, Mr. Joseph, Shotley Bridge, 1 copy.
Surtees, Mr. John, Co-operative Store, Consett, 1 copy.
Surtees, Mr. Wm., Benfieldside, 1 copy.
Surtees, Mr. Thomas, Co-operative Store, Shotley Bridge, 1 copy.
Surtees, Mr. Geo., Wheldon's House, Ebchester, 1 copy.
Surtees, Mr. Jos. L., 19, Sherburn Terrace, Consett, 1 copy.
Swan, Robert, Esq., 95, Roker Avenue, Sunderland, 1 copy.
Swaby, Rev. Wm. Proctor, S. Mark's Vicarage, Millfield, Sunder-
    land, 1 copy.
Swinburn, Mr. J. T., Black House, Shotley Bridge, 1 copy.
Sykes, Rev. E. S., M.A., curate of St. John's, Sunderland, 2 copies.

ℭ

Tait, Mr. John, 23, Sherburn Terrace, Consett, 1 copy.
Taylor, Mr. Edward, Benfieldside, 1 copy.
Taylor, Mr. Robert, The Terrace, Shotley Bridge, 1 copy.
Taylor, Mr. W. R., Stanifordam, Consett, 1 copy.
Taylor, Mr. J. B., High Pittington, Durham, 1 copy.
Taylor, Mr. Isaac, 9, Millicent Terrace, Gateshead, 1 copy.
Taylor, Mr. Henry, 76, Gilesgate, Durham, 1 copy.
Teare, Mr. P., Board Schools, Benfieldside, 1 copy.
Telford, Mr. Thomas, 18, Wharncliffe Street, Newcastle, 1 copy.
Telford, Mr. Robert, Berry Edge Farm, Consett, 1 copy.
Telford, Mr. W., Cutlers' Hall, Benfieldside, 1 copy.
Temperley, Mr. Wm., Edmondbyers, 1 copy.
Templeton, Mr. S., 4, Bessemer Street, Blackhill, 1 copy.
Thirlwell, Mr. John, Snod's Edge, Blackhill, 2 copies.
Thirlwell, Mr. John, Front Street, Shotley Bridge, 1 copy.
Thirlwell, Mr. Joshua, 12, Allendale Cottages, 1 copy.
Thompson, Thomas C., Esq., M.P., 1, Lower Grosvenor Place,
    London, 1 copy.
Thompson, Mr. James, Sherburn, Durham, 1 copy.
Thompson, Mr. Wm., Cutlers' Hall, Shotley Bridge, 1 copy.
Thompson, Mr. Jas., 42, Cloth Market, Newcastle-on-Tyne, 1 copy.
Thompson, Mr. Joseph, Post Office, Shotley Bridge, 1 copy.
Thompson, Mr. John J., Prentice Close House, Lanchester, 1 copy.
Thompson, Mrs. Brewster, 15, Grosvenor Terrace, Harrogate, 1
    copy.
Thompson, Mr. Thos., Exchange Buildings, Ramsgate, Stockton-
    on-Tees, 1 copy.

Thompson, Mr. James, registrar, Lanchester, 1 copy.
Thubron, Mr. John, 53, Derwent Road, Gateshead, 1 copy.
Tilly, Mr. Wm., Blackhill, 1 copy.
Tooby, Mr. Geo., 166, Jefferson Street, Newcastle-on-Tyne, 1 copy.
Town, Annandale, Esq., J.P., Allansford, 1 copy.
Tregelles, Edwin O., Esq., Banbury, 1 copy.
Tregenza, Mr. P. P., Malwda Walks, Sheffield, 1 copy.
Trotter, Mr. Andrew, Shotley Grove, Shotley Bridge, 1 copy.
Tucker, Mr. John, 6, Belgrave Terrace, Gateshead, 1 copy.
Turner, Mr. George, 3, Dixon Street, Blackhill, 1 copy.
Turner, Mr. Wm., Whitehall Lodge, Blackhill, 1 copy.
Turner, Mr. A. E., 41, Durham Road, Blackhill, 1 copy.
Turner, Mr. Chas., 35, Cromwell Street, Newcastle, 1 copy.
Turnbull, Mr. Thos., Whittonstall Woodhouse, Stocksfield, 1 copy.

U

Uncles, Mr. Henry, Wood Street, Shotley Bridge, 1 copy.
Uytman, Mr. John, 20, Church Street, Johnstone, near Glasgow,
    1 copy.
Urwin, Mr. Wm., Front Street, Shotley Bridge, 1 copy.
Urwin, Mr. James, New Pittington, Durham, 1 copy.
Urwin, Mr. L., Front Street, Shotley Bridge, 1 copy.
Urwin, Robt., Esq., St. Nicholas' Buildings, Newcastle, 2 copies.

V

Vasey, Miss, Market Place, Durham, 1 copy.

W

Walker, E. J., Esq., Shotley House, Shotley Bridge, 1 copy.
Walker, Miss V., Shotley House, Shotley Bridge, 1 copy.
Walker & Emley, Messrs., Westgate Road, Newcastle, 2 copies.
Walton, Mr. Ralph, Bessemer Street, Blackhill, 1 copy.
Walton, Mr. Ralph, Lanchester, Durham, 1 copy.
Ward, Mr. Wm., Iveston, 1 copy.
Ward, Mr. Wm., Shotley Grove, Shotley Bridge, 1 copy.
Wardhaugh, Mr. W., Front Street, Shotley Bridge, 1 copy.
Wardhaugh, Mr. E., High Street, Sunderland, 1 copy.
Wardhaugh, Mr. W., Junr., Front Street, Shotley Bridge, 1 copy.
Wardhaugh, Mr. E., Jun., blacksmith, Shotley Bridge, 1 copy.
Wardhaugh, Mrs., Baxton Burn, Blackhill, 1 copy.
Wardle, Mr. John, Low Westwood, Ebchester, 1 copy.

Wardle, Mr John, Ebchester, 1 copy.
Watson, Mr. G., Whitley N. School, Hexham, 2 copies.
Watson, Mr. H. W., Burnopfield, 1 copy.
Watson, Mr. T., Wesleyan preacher, Consett, 1 copy.
Waugh, Mr. Geo., Low Waskerley, Shotley Bridge, 1 copy.
Waugh, Mr. T., Low Waskerley, Shotley Bridge, 1 copy.
Wayman, J. W., Esq., Mayor of Sunderland, 1 copy.
Wheatley, Mr. W., Shotley Bridge, 1 copy.
Wheatley, Mr. W., veterinary surgeon, 23, Saville Street, South
        Shields, 1 copy.
Wheldon, Miss, Shotley Villa, Shotley Bridge, 1 copy.
Whinney, Mr. Thomas, Cemetery Lodge, Blackhill, 1 copy.
White, Mr. Joseph, Sherburn Hill, Durham, 1 copy.
Whiteley, Mr. Alfred, Lightcliffe, Halifax, 1 copy.
Whitfield, Messrs. & Sons, Winlaton, Blaydon, 1 copy.
Wilbraham, A. B., Esq., Snow's Green House, Shotley Bridge, 1 copy.
Wiles, Mr. Wm., Sherburn Terrace, Consett, 1 copy.
Wilkinson, Mr. John, Morrowfield, Chester-le-Street, 1 copy.
Wilson, Mr. W., Oakfield, Shotley Bridge, 1 copy.
Willis, Rev. R. G., Goodmanham, Market Weighton, Yorks., 1
        copy.
Willey, Mr. Aaron, Ebchester, 1 copy.
Williams, Mr. R. B., Blackhill, 1 copy.
Wilson, Mr. George, Springfield, Shotley Bridge, 1 copy.
Wilson, John, Esq., M.D., Lanchester, 1 copy.
Wilson, Mr. Robert, 29, Argyle Street, Glasgow, 1 copy.
Wilson, Mr. Geo., Shotley Hall, Shotley Bridge, 1 copy.
Wilson, Charles, Esq., Shotley Park, Shotley Bridge, 1 copy.
Wilson, Mr. John, 27, Front Street, Shotley Bridge, 1 copy.
Wilson, Mr. Henry, 73, Clayton Street, Newcastle, 1 copy.
Wilson, Mr. Wm., Jun., Oak Street, Shotley Bridge, 1 copy.
Wilson, Mr., exciseman, Lanchester, 1 copy.
Wilson, Mr., Shotley Hall, Shotley Bridge, 1 copy.
Wood, Mr. Jas. H., Field Head, Shotley Bridge, 1 copy.
Wood, Miss, Springfield, Shotley Bridge, 1 copy.
Wood, Miss Rebecca, Springfield, Shotley Bridge, 1 copy.
Woodman, Mr. George, Norfolk Street, Sunderland, 1 copy.
Wright, Mr. W. H., East Castle, Leadgate, 1 copy.
Wright, Mr. James, 8, Roger Street, Blackhill, 1 copy.

Y

Yuile, Mr., Shotley, Shotley Bridge, 1 copy.
Young, Mr. Wm., Durham Road, Blackhill, 1 copy.

Yours faithfully

W Jenkins.

Stanzas to her Majesty, Queen Victoria.

LADY, the noblest of your favoured reign
 With trembling speak the merits of their Queen,
 Lest all-impotent be their feeble strain
 To breathe the praises due ; much less, I ween,
Should one, your humblest subject, be so vain
As bind his thoughts, though love-inspired, in rhyme :
He had not thus have shown so bold a mien,
Had not a volume in Victoria's time
Seemed, lacking her bright name, a sun-forsaken clime.

Recalling infancy, Victoria's name
First pressed the tender tablets of my heart,
And deeply has it written there its claim
To that deep reverence which a mother taught ;
The honour is not mine : the patriot thought
Was breathed into my being e'er to dwell.
Afar in other realms I've roved, and caught
Its echoes like to distant music's swell,
Which wooed my bosom back to shores it loved so well.

B

Happy, O glorious England, thou art now!
A monarch rules by virtue swayed ;—and ne'er
Did thy proud crown sit on a worthier brow,
Where smiling freedom mocks the tyrant's sneer,
And pity dwells, to misery ever dear;
And leaps within her shrine when kindred woe˙
Goes through the land, and mourners shed the tear—
The thrilling tear, bereavement bids to flow
To quench the glowing joy that happier days bestow.

Happy, O Albion! for in this alone
Thou art more blest than other lands may be ;
It is not in the splendour of a throne,
Which sheds its glory over earth and sea,
That honour finds an immortality :
'Tis that religion's light is shining there,
Pointing a radiant pathway to the sky,
Dispensed with woman's tenderness and care,—
O Virtue, Honour, Truth, what triumphs you may share !

When o'er the land the gloom of sorrow came,
From legion hearts the smile of joy to chase,
When he succumbed to death whose honoured name
Keeps in the hearts of men its wonted place,
Lady, " o'er him who uttered nothing base,"
With you the nation poured its warmest tears,
And time shall ne'er that sympathy erase ;
The patriot father, who that name reveres,
Shall tell it to his child to ring through countless years.

A noble spirit ! such his spouse hath been :
If patriot rapture did his breast inspire,
'Twas nursed within the bosom of his Queen,
To burn as burns Vesuvius' quenchless fire.
If England's morals have not mounted higher
Towards the haven of some purer clime,
And marked the age with deeds the good admire,
It is not that her monarch smiled on crime,
But rather taught the heart to ponder things sublime.

In other climes, far o'er the booming seas,
Wherever Britain's name is heard to ring,
(And is there one lone spot of earth whose breeze
Has not been vocal with its echoing?)
Victoria's name is as a magic thing,
Flinging enchantments o'er the hearts of men;
The savage dreams its power, lingering
By waving forest, mountain, crag, and glen,
And blesses freedom's home and Albion's glorious Queen.

The sable son of Afric's torrid zone,
The slave of tyranny's desire for gold,
Looks to our shore with bosom-rending groan
And asks, with pity, why he's bought and sold?
Lady, no fault is yours; the Briton bold
Would have the world as mountain breezes, free!
Brave Livingstone! thou of heroic mould,
The fettered millions look with hope to thee:
Urge on thy soul's desire till crowned by victory.

Thou art no fabled child of fevered thought,
And he who seeks a thrilling tale to tell
To glowing hearts of future ages, fraught
With all the varied elements which swell
The human breast, may turn to thee and dwell
On deeds illumed by Truth's eternal light:
And if his genius fit the subject well,
It will be shown the best and bravest fight
Without the sword or shield, save heaven's protecting might.

So, lady, God your sword and shield hath been;—
In vain the wretch has sought your blood to spill,
To take a life the millions love, I ween;
But pistols err, nor men have power to kill
Whom God protects, escape the flashing steel,
And tempests howling through the sounding sky;
The toppling crags, winds, waves, obey His will:
To such in vain do danger's arrows fly,
For guided by His hand, they harmlessly pass by.

Blest be the children of your house and heart,
And whereso'er their fields of labour lie ;
May that fair wisdom ne'er their souls desert,
Taught and impressed beneath a parent's eye.
And O ! may virtue ever linger by,
And guide them safely through the snares of earth,
To breathe the blessing which shall never die,
And emulate their parents' deeds and worth ;
Whilst, lady, from our hearts this wish we would pour forth :

O ! long may she, the Mother of the Isles,
Bless her brave children with a mother's care,
Throw o'er our homes the sunshine of her smiles,
And reign a welcome guardian angel there ;
Beloved of the nations, may she spare
Our tears through long and happy years to come,
And though her brow the widow's wreath may wear,
Which points, like autumn's seer leaves, to the tomb,
Her virtue's lights shall shine like starbeams 'mid the gloom.

"Come with me to yon bridge that spans the flood,
For here a charming landscape meets the eye."

The Bridge at Shotley.

Shotley Bridge.*

NO sounding domes, which echo to the tread,
    Nor towers majestic rear their forms on high,—
    Nor ancient palace lifts its sombre head,
       To kiss the blue or brave the stormy sky,—
Hast thou, sweet village ; but where'er the eye
   'Turns in its musings, Beauty greets the sight ;—
Whether upon the shining river by,
    When pale Diana pours her flood of light,
And mortals love with awe beneath the tranquil night ;

---

* Shotley Bridge is situated on the right bank of the river Derwent, at an equal distance of fourteen miles from Newcastle, Durham, and Hexham. The Derwent here divides the counties of Durham and Northumberland, and is spanned by a bridge of one arch, or, more correctly speaking, of two arches of the same form and dimension put up at different times ; the western one, much older of the two, having been found too narrow for convenient traffic, the eastern part was added about sixty years ago. A bridge evidently existed here five or six hundred years ago, for in the survey of Bishop Hatfield, we find under Benfieldside, one of the vills of the Manor of Lanchester, William Broune holding 1 messuage and 12 acres, formerly held by William at the Brig ; and, again, Thomas of the Brig held 1 messuage and 27 acres, formerly held by John Abell. It may be assumed, however, from the fact of a ford existing at Shotley until comparatively recent times, that the bridge was a wooden structure for foot passengers only. The engraving on the opposite page represents the bridge as it appeared in 1838, since which time the surroundings have undergone but slight alteration. The view from this point is exceedingly picturesque, whether you look up or down the river. Immediately above the bridge, the river dashes over a ledge of millstone grit, through which the water has cut numerous channels, into a pool, known as "Jenny's Hole," from which many a noble trout has been taken in days gone by, when the adjoining hostelry of the Bridge Inn was a famous and favourite

Or on the landscape, where wood, field, and glen
  Vie in their wealth of loveliness, and smile
As things of human mind on wayward men,
  To draw them forth from error, and beguile
The lower passions.   Virtue's free the while,
  Calling the heart to objects more divine.
Alas ! that sin the meanest breast should soil,
  Since mother Nature is a holy shrine
Of purity and joy : partake and ne'er repine.

resort for anglers.   From the bridge to the Paper Mill, higher up the stream, the banks on both sides are overhung with beech and oak, and the river has formed its bed in the millstone grit, which it has laid bare. This rock, as its name implies, has long been used for millstones, for which, from its extreme hardness, it is peculiarly adapted.   That such has been its use in this locality five centuries ago, the records to be presently referred to conclusively prove.   The earliest mention of Shotley Bridge by name is in an admittance of Gilbert de Brendon to " one acre of new waste which lies near the high street which leads to Shotley Brigg," rendering 6*d.* yearly, recorded in the Halmote Roll of the Manor of Lanchester, under Benfieldside, 11th Hatfield (1356).   In the same Roll, in the 11th year of Bishop Skirlaw, (1399), John Robinson is fined for not having John Milner of Iveston to answer the Lord for five millstones obtained at Shotle Brig ; and at a subsequent Court (vol. 3, p. 571) the jury of the vill of Benfieldside present that " John Sadler arrested John Milner of Ilhestane (Iveston) for two pairs of millstones, of the value of two shillings, for the Lord's rent for leave to dig the millstones in the Lord's soil near Shotle Brig."   The Halmote Rolls contain numerous entries of payments made for license to dig millstones out of the bed of the river, and frequent fines are inflicted for taking them without the Lord's license.   John, the Miller of Iveston, was not the only offender.   Thomas Brown is fined 4*d.* for taking a pair of quernstones without leave (p. 300).   At the same Court, John of Iveston is amerced in 6*d.* for a small millstone, for the payment of which the said Thomas Brown, though trespasser himself, is not refused as his surety. It is curious to observe traces of these depredations upon the Lord's strict rights still existing in the river bed, after the lapse of five centuries. Between the bridge and the Paper Mill, may be seen numerous round holes in the millstone grit, from which millstones have been taken ; and as in some places the slow action of the water on this hard rock has almost worn away the trace of the holes from which it is evident millstones at a remote period have been removed, it is not difficult to believe that the entries above refer to some of the existing marks.   The accompanying woodcut is taken from a sketch by Richardson, and will convey an idea of the village near 50 years ago, before the transition from rural retirement into a species of surhurban town had commenced.   Now, however, the slopes above the village are covered with handsome villas, whose sites have been well chosen, and whose architectural characteristics harmonise with the features of the adjoining landscape.—*History of West Durham.*

Shotley Bridge in 1840.

Reader, deem not the soul which gladly lingers
  By Beauty's dwellings, in the flower or tree,
Whose glorious tints are touched by peerless fingers,
  Or the still shining lake or surging sea,
Looks not through these upon Eternity,
  Or worships beauty in a narrow sense
For her sweet sake alone, for it is free
  To trace the limitless intelligence,—
Who made the hallowed lovelier things, that thence

Mankind might quaff the spirit of His lore ;
  And thus, with other aid, their souls might climb
To His high altar on a purer shore,
  And breathe the love and majesty sublime,
Which live in vigour in that stainless clime,
  Where Hunger, Sin, and Hate can have no home.
O God ! that man should choose the curse of crime,
  And give within his breast the viper room,
Whose sting can poison here, and damn him in the tomb.

Here, in these shades, in Summer's genial air,
  'Mid gardens sloping toward the river's shore,
Are flowers as fragrant, blushing maids as fair,
  As Eastern clime can boast, or gods adore.
Here may the gloomy poet dream his lore,
  Where nought save man blots Nature's comely face,
And hear in sounds, the river's dashing roar,
  The full-voiced winds, the song-bird's gushing praise,
The spirit-notes of Him whose being fills all space.

Come roam with me, my friend, and we will share
  The tender pleasures of a waking dream.
First, let us to the Hally Well repair,—
  Thou art, I think, a stranger to my theme.
Here, many years ago, a man supreme
  In mind and wealth among his fellows round,
Raised yon fair cots which in the sun-light gleam,—
  That humble shed by moss-grown heather crowned,
Whence flows a copious spring of water from the ground.

Here quaffed the scurvy-smitten ones of yore,
  And praised the merits of the healing flood,
The breeze, but still the benefactor more,*
  And grew in ardour as their health grew good ;†
But he who labouring for the public stood
  Admired, respected, loved, is slighted now ;—
A seeming error raised the multitude,
  And those who shared his bounty most, I vow,
Remember all his faults, his virtues ne'er allow.

* Jonathan Richardson, who projected and carried into execution those great improvements that have quite changed the general aspect of Shotley Bridge. He was connected with the Durham and Northumberland District Bank at the time of its failure in 1857, and he was blamed by some for the unfortunate occurrence, which brought poverty to many a previously happy home ; but that the accusations laid to his charge were groundless has many a time ere this been proved.—*History of West Durham.*

† From the earliest ages, men have placed a high value upon mineral waters, as possessing divine remedies for various diseases which afflict mankind. The common well, in many oriental countries, was viewed as of vital importance, simply because of the value of water in their arid climate ; and especially in the wilderness a spring was viewed as a direct bounty of Providence, because it was necessary to the preservation of life, and hence called "the living water," or the water of life. But where the waters of a spring either constantly, or recurrently at certain periods, were known to have some healing properties, there arose in the minds of the people a more immediate recognition of divine purpose, and an increased veneration. Our Saxon forefathers, also, according to the customs of the ancients, had their sacred fountains, especially such as were thought to have healing virtues, and from them we have derived the name "Hally Well." Some have written the name "Holy Well," and supposed "Hally Well" to be a corruption or provincialism ; but, as a matter of fact, the common people preserve the original of names longer than the learned. Hally is the adjective form of the Saxon word *hal,* meaning sound in bodily health ; and, secondly, sound in a moral sense. The hally well, therefore, was no doubt so denominated while the Saxon was the mother tongue of the common people. "Spa" is the name of a town in Belgium, famed for its medicinal waters, and is now generally given to all mineral springs ; hence the name has been applied to the mineral waters of Shotley. Tradition points out a hally well at Shotley from time immemorial, and its water was always thought to be remedial in scrofulous complaints. An old inhabitant, who was wont to court the Muses, has fairly well expressed the received opinion in these lines—

"No scurvy in your skin can dwell,
  If you only drink the Hally Well."

In the beginning of this century, there were those in the village who could remember their juvenile sports around the spring, where they used

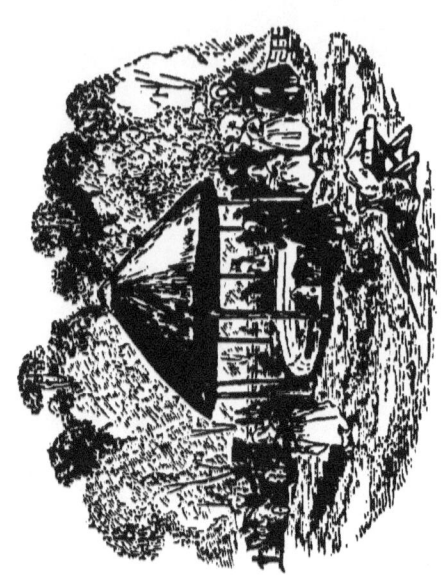

" That humble shed, by moss-grown heather crowned,
Whence flows a copious spring of water from the ground."

The Daily Well.

But Time's old car majestically rolled on,
    Correcting error, showing fallacy ;
And men of narrower sense than Richardson,
    See now the vision as he saw with eye,
Whose glance prescient read the Future's sky,
    Which canopied the world's commercial maze :
Had Honour not been forced the field to fly,
    As cursed Mistrust looked on with withering gaze,
Men had not wronged him then, nor spared till now their praise.

to drink for the purpose of seeing each other's grimaces at the taste. Many people at that time from distant places used to frequent the well to drink the water, and carry away supplies for use at home. The water used to stand in a natural basin formed by surrounding hillocks of moss and grass, the quantity never seeming to vary. The water having formed a sort of bog, was drained away into the Derwent ; and it was noticed that the sides of the channel in which the water flowed were always of a vermilion colour, indicating the presence of a considerable quantity of iron. Such, according to Mr. Ryan's History of Shotley Spa, to which interesting little work we are indebted for many of the foregoing details, was the condition of the well about seventy-five years ago. The time, however, was to come when the valuable spring was to be made more widely known. In 1838, Mr. Jonathan Richardson, the owner of the estate, made a search for the source of the once famous mineral water, and under the guidance of some old inhabitants he succeeded in finding the hally well. There was, however, much to be done in order to bring the Spa into deserved notoriety, and to make the situation suitable for a health resort. But, confident in the high value of the mineral spring, he immediately undertook the necessary improvements and erections required, and his energy and liberality, seldom surpassed, soon made every arrangement for the accommodation of visitors to Shotley Spa. An upright stone was placed over the well, and the water was made to flow through a spout into a round, low basin, as in the accompanying woodcut, which depicts the well surrounded by visitors to the Spa, and which is reproduced from a sketch made by Richardson in 1838. A saloon and bathroom were erected a short distance off, carriage drives and footpaths were formed, and soon the estate resembled an ornamental garden. To the south-east of the Spa, and in close proximity, a handsome hotel, planned on a large scale, with a suitable set of stables, was built ; and other residences starting into existence at the same time for the accommodation of the visitors who flocked to the place, the general aspect of the village rapidly changed. The Spa is about half-a-mile from the town, and is surrounded by some romantic scenery. After passing through the lodge gates, a broad walk or carriage road winding under a lofty canopy of trees, leads you towards the Spa, and round the haughs in which it is situated. The visitor will then observe that he has entered a natural park, and treads on the arena, or rather the meadow-floor of a vast ampitheatre, formed by the graceful circumvolution of the banks towering around ; the trees, of rich and varied foliage, and rising above each

Thou hast, companion of my way, an eye
   For Heaven's Creations—Nature's loveliness.
Look eastward on that scene's sublimity,
   · That emerald mantled beauteous precipice ;
The cloud-aspiring trees, with fond caress
   The zephyrs woo them.   Mark their graceful motion :
Wave piled on wave receding might impress   ·
   Thy breast that thou wert gazing on an ocean
With endless hues adorned, in proud and wild devotion.

A few steps onward, I have yet to show
   Thine eyes delighted, an enchanting dell ;
The sunbeams peep into its depths below,
   In whose soft light the shadowy glories dwell.
Here the calm-loving fern a tale may tell,
   And woo thee from distraction to repose ;
The moss-grown rock, the flower, the streamlet's swell,
   Preach each their sermon, breathing joys and woes,
Shall raise thy tender soul to Love's volcanic throes.

     There are whom beauty cannot thrill,
       Nor love to aught ecstatic wake,—
     Who see nought glorious in the rill,
       The silver saugh or shining lake,—
     Who walk by fields of starry flowers,
     Or sylvan nooks, or twilight bowers,—
     Or where the mountains' craggy forms,
     Bury their heads in clouds and storms,
     Or kiss the far inviting blue
     'Mid freshest air and purest dew,—   '
     Or by the roaring waterfalls,
     Where echo unto echo calls,—
     Without a wonder, sigh, or thought
       Of whence all came, what hand had given,
     And cold as marble feel for nought,
     Who weep not, glow not, are not fraught
      · With living light, which flows from heaven.

other on the valley sides, will appear as innumerable spectators. Around
the area of this ampitheatre, the carriage-road, pleasingly curved, runs
more than a mile,—sometimes skirting the wood, and again going under
its canopy,—sometimes being inflected by the Derwent's pebbled channel,
and again allowing a pleasant plantation to hide the beauty and increase
the musical ripple of the stream.—*History of West Durham,*

Such men may walk the battle plain
Where nations' saviours fought, in vain ;
They climb the Alps, with quaking fear,
For what ? to say they've ventured there,
But feel no thrill for majesty
Investing every feature by ;
The smiling vale reposed beneath,
As sweet as joy, and calm as death ;
Whilst far above, in glancing light
The snowpack rears its stainless white,
Evincing purity is given
Proportioned to the height it soars :
The whiter still, the nearer heaven—
Perfection seeks celestial shores.

Enough ! we'll bend our way along the river,
And view the waters glide, and fume, and glance,
As on their chainless course they roll for ever,
And to their self-made music lilting dance ;
Now glittering sheen, beneath the blue expanse
Of Heaven's glory in its noontide glare ;
Now nursing quivering moonbeams as they prance,
Now mirroring deep the canopy of air
Begemmed with " Isles of light," so wonderful and fair.

This quiet village wooes our gaze again,
And breathes felicity along the shore.
Give me thine ear, I will its tale explain :
Here (when the rod of persecution bore
On Luther's converts, and their souls no more
Could bear the pressure of the tyrant's will)
Fled many an artizan,* who dug the ore,
Which fell to shapes obedient to their skill ;
The polished sword and knife flashed from the busy mill.

---

* The history of Shotley Bridge, as a place of importance, may be said
to have commenced at the close of the seventeenth century, when it was
colonized by a few German refugees, who fled from their own country for
the sake of religious liberty. The Shotley colonists came from Solingen,

Here hummed with hollow roar the water-wheel,
　　As hissed the blade upon the circling stone ;
'There clashed the hammer with the sparkling steel ;
　　The sounding anvil rang with bell-like tone.
Skill reared for memory an immortal throne,
　　And Derwent's waters rivalled Tagus' fame.
Now the last anvil's silent and alone ;
　　The Mill has an existence but in name,
And death has all from whence the deeds of genius came.

a small city of Cleve Berg, in Germany, celebrated of old for cutlery manufactures. Their names, as far as can be ascertained with any degree of certainty, were Oley, Vooz, Mole, and Bertram. The account of their choosing this locality preserved among their descendants is that they sought for a place suited to their purpose in several parts of England, especially near the metropolis ; but wanting to conceal the secret of their excellence in tempering and some other mysteries of their art, they sought a *locus standi* on the Tyne, and not having found one there, they commenced to explore the Derwent, following the course of the river until they reached Shotley, where the remarkable softness of the water, the excellence of the ironstone in the neighbouring hills, and no doubt the seclusion of the spot, induced them to terminate their pilgrimage. Situated thus during the long continental wars, having abundant orders, the Germans, and especially the Oleys, the principal proprietors, enjoyed a long-continued flow of prosperity. Their swords equalled in flexibility, strength, and elegance the distinguished blades of Damascus and Toledo. As an instance of their skill, it is related that one of the sword-makers, Robert Oley, who left Shotley Bridge at the beginning of this century, made a wager with eight foremen smiths that he would produce within a fortnight a spring which should excel any · they might make. At the expiration of the stated time, Oley appeared at the place of meeting, but apparently without the spring. He was at once declared to have lost the wager. Coolly placing his hat on the table, Oley announced that his spring was there, and asked some one to take it out of the hat. None, however, complied with the request, for the spring which lay coiled up in the hat was a fine, double-edged sword. Oley himself now took out the sword, and then offered to pay the amount of the wager to anyone who could tell which way the weapon had been coiled, but no one was able to do so. A portion of the sword-mill used by the Germans is still standing on the right bank of the river, near the bridge. Several of the houses which they occupied bore inscriptions at the early part of the present century, which told the cause of the sword-makers leaving their fatherland, but the most of these inscriptions are now altogether illegible or partly effaced. Above the doorway of an old two-storied house, once the property of the Oleys, and now owned by the Messrs Annandale, there is a stone inserted, bearing an inscription in German, dated 1691. By those who know the language, the following is considered to be a good translation :—
" The blessing of the Lord makes rich without care, so long as you are

Yes, those brave colonists brought useful arts,*
  And through their genius gave our valley fame.
Theirs was the high-born principle that darts
  Through Freedom's bosoms, as the quenchless flame
Bursts forth from Etna, which no despot's name
  Nor threat, nor vengence for an hour can mar,
Nor crush into obedience, nor tame ;
  No ! when the tyrant's dust is scattered far,
Fair Freedom's fires shall burn and dazzle like a star.

In that gray pile, now lit with Summer's ray,
  Some thoughtful boy or hoary Christian sire,
When toil gave place to rest with dying day,
  No doubt rehearsed the stories round the fire,
How the poor lad (the mark of Popish ire)
  Sang in the streets his sweetest hymns for bread,
With that deep pathos sorrow can inspire,
  Till sympathetic Cotta had him led
Unto her home, and saw her young guest clothed and fed.

industrious in your vocation, and do what is ordered you." At the close
of Napoleon's era of wars, the demand for swords diminished, and what
was once a flourishing industry soon afterwards ceased altogether. Many
of the old German families have become extinct, or are lost in other
family names, but some remain beside the Oley family, and in particular
several families of the Moles—originally written Moll—whose ancestor,
it is said, appropriately with his name as now pronounced, came over
to this country covered up in a tub.—*History of West Durham.*

  * The Oleys were sword-makers, the Moles sword-grinders, the Vooz'
traded between Germany and England, and the Bertrams were steel
manufacturers at Blackhall Mill, about three-and-a-half-miles below
Shotley Bridge. A forge of theirs stood on the site of a neat cottage
occupied by Mr. Campbell, the property of the very worthy and enterprising gentlemen, the Messrs. Annandale, on the left bank of the
Derwent, just above their High Paper Mill ; and about a mile further
up the river, on the same side, near Allansford, are the remains of an
old furnace, which probably had been used by the Bertrams. The
effect of the extreme heat can yet be traced on the glazed stones. A
few yards from this pile, up a steep acclivity to the west, are three
ruinous kilns, where the ironstone appears to have been put through its
first process—roasting. The shape of the furnace had been hexagonal,
narrowing towards the top ; that of the kilns round, narrowing towards
the bottom.

Or how the hero of immortal mind,
　　In solitary grandeur stood before
The mighty throng at Worms, whose ranks combined
　　The Emperor, Judge, Duke, Prince, Ambassador,
Magnificent and awful, yet he bore
　　The dauntless brow of changeless Truth e'en there ;
Disclosed he then his eagle thoughts to soar,
　　And left a Christian conqueror to share
A lot the glorious sons of Light must ever dare.

Thou know'st, my friend, of Luther, and may'st deem
　　Those German Christians nursed his thoughts, and fanned
Their patriot fires when he became their theme
　　In turning to their much-loved fatherland ;
For home has aye a power at her command—
　　A witchery about her naught excels :
Her mountains are the loveliest that stand
　　Beneath high heaven ; her woodlands, streams, and dells,
And maidens ever wear a thousand starry spells.

A halo cinctures the enchanting spot
　　Where we are born, which, as the years roll on,
Gathers in radiance whatsoe'er our lot,—
　　The humble cot, the palace or the throne.
If thou hast wandered in another zone,
　　Far from thy native hills and valleys fair,
This truth thou'st learnt, which death can blot alone
　　From out thy breast, and thought the sunshine there
Less cheering than the clouds known to thy country dear.

Hence, this is fitting passion to disclose,
　　For Pity wakes and thrills thy breast and mine
When poring on the exiles' wrongs and woes,
　　Who wept, but dared not seek their lovely Rhine ;
Their sorrows were not fruitless : a divine
　　And holy purpose was their guiding light ;
The bud they cherished has become a vine,
　　Which breathes to every clime a wild delight,
And every home may know its comfort-giving might.

Come with me to yon bridge that spans the flood,
  For here a charming landscape meets the eye,
Where oft in adoration I have stood
  And listened to the twilight breezes sigh
Like human voices soft and feelingly ;
  And mused upon the graceful trees reclining,
Wooing the gentle waters gliding by,
  Like maids with loose locks o'er a mirror shining,
A conquest of some heart with woman's skill designing.

Behold that channelled rock ! could sculptor's art
  Copy its rude sublimity ? where brawl
The twisting currents ; with delirious start
  They fuming leap the tiny waterfall.
List the soft echoes to each other call,
  The hollow moaning, and the hissing sound :
Well might'st thou think the elements were all
  Peopled with being, passionate but bound,
And harmless in their strife, yet solemn and profound.

I would that thou had'st lingered here with me,
  When winter walked relentless through the wood,
And seen the snow glance on each leafless tree ;
  The sunbeams darting through the fissured cloud,
Falling upon the feathered branch and flood,
  Giving innumerable mimic stars to earth,
Which smiled and glanced in seeming gratitude,
  Thanking their parent for their radiant birth,
Thy feeling heart, I know, in joyance had gone forth.

    The sounds which thou to rapture fire,
      And o'er the valley glide,
    Flow from yon heavenward pointing spire
      Upon the green hill side.

    St. Cuthbert's bells, as shadows creep
      Along the twilight lea,
    Make glad the sombre hour, and steep
      The ear in melody.

Thou'st felt the magic power of sound ;—
  When first those bells, 'tis said,
Rushed on the limpid air around,
  And woke the sunny glade,

The lark, in her aerial home,
  Poised as the humming bird
Above the honeysuckle's bloom,
  And charmed to silence heard.

The thrush and linnet ceased their lay,
  The black-bird's echoing strain
No longer trembled thro' the spray,
  Or quavered o'er the plain.

The hare from out her native dell
  Came skipping to the sounds,
Nor felt the fear-inspired spell
  Of huntsmen and of hounds.

The troutlet, to the trembling roll,
  Which o'er the waters played,
Disported in his favourite pool
  As if by magic's aid.

But thou and I must part, my friend,
  Thy patience serves thee well ;
When next thou would'st thy soul unbend
From meaner things, oh ! may it end
  As calm as this. Farewell !

Hallgarth.*

COME, stir my soul, thou welcome Melancholy—
   Friend and inspirer of my tenderest strains,
   Companion of my wand'rings, free from folly,
   Through the deep dells, by waterfalls, o'er plains,
Where the enchantress, Solitude, remains,
   And wields her spell-fraught wand o'er those who seek
Her throne amid the flowers of her domains;
   Where Echo talks her lore, and warblers speak
A language full of soul—Love's pathos never weak.

* Hallgarth is the name of that central part of the parish of Pittington which was anciently called the Manor *(manerium)* of the Monks of Durham, to whom the whole parish belonged. It was usually held in the Prior's hands as the demesne of the Abbey, instead of being leased to tenants, as other parts of the parish were. In it the Parish Church is situated, which is consequently known in the locality as Hallgarth Church, the parish itself being also often spoken of as Hallgarth parish. The name is doubtless derived from "Prior's Hall," which formerly stood in a plot of ground, now a garden, north of the Churchyard, "garth" meaning the surrounding enclosure. This "Prior's Hall" was a building for the occasional residence of the Prior of Durham, and for holding of courts, with chambers for monks, and with extensive farm buildings round it. Ruins of the Hall built in the sixteenth century by Hugh Whitehead, the last Prior and first Dean of Durham, remained in the aforesaid plot of ground, which is still called "Prior's Garth," till recent times. Hallgarth Church, which is one of the most interesting in the county, may be concluded to stand on the site of an earlier Saxon one; for there can be little doubt that Pittington was an

Oft, Melancholy, hast thou tinged my thought,
In boyish musings by this sombre pile ;
When the rich landscape was with beauty fraught,
Whose starry flowers seemed on me to smile
As creatures sensitive whom pleasures guile ;
Or hang their heads with mine on pensive woe,
And, thrilling, weep their dewy tears the while,
In kindred pity for some friend laid low,
To whom fond memory clings, and never shall forego.

Years long, not many, o'er my head have passed
Since on this scene of youth, hope, sorrow, bliss,
I gazed.   In other lands Iv'e roved, nor cast
My eye on aught that charmed it like to this ;
The stream, whose trembling waves the flowers kiss
With lips of redolency, fair with rays,—
The Church, throned on a mound of loveliness,—
The tombs, where soft light falls, and Pity strays,—
The meads and pastures,—beautiful beyond all praise ;

ancient Saxon settlement long before the Norman Conquest, and
before the monks of Lindisfarne settled finally at Durham, and built
their Abbey there.   But of such early church no traces remain, or
at any rate have been so far discovered,—unless it be a sun-dial,
now built into the southern wall of the Church, which has been
pronounced by competent authority to be Saxon.   The earliest part
of the present Church may be assigned to a date not later than
A.D. 1100.   But it has been added to and otherwise altered at
various later times.   The north aisle, with its beautiful round
Norman arches, may have been added about A.D. 1150 ; the pointed
arches of the south aisle, in what is called the Early English style,
mark a later addition.   Till the year 1846, the original Norman
chancel arch remained, beyond which was a long chancel of the
Early English period.   But in the year above mentioned, restoration
(often complained of by antiquaries as demolition) was undertaken.
The old chancel was pulled down, the nave and aisles were prolonged
eastward to the extent of one additional arch on each side, a new
chancel arch was made, and the present short chancel erected
beyond it.   Thus the original proportions of the Church were
destroyed, and interesting features may have been swept away.
But it is a Church both beautiful and interesting still, the arcade
of the northern aisle, with the zigzag mouldings of its arches, and
the unique spiral ornamentation of its columns, being admired by
all beholders as peculiarly effective.   For its venerable beauty, no
less than for the associations that surround it, well worthy is old
Hallgarth Church of the reverent affection with which it is regarded
by the parishioners.

Nursing the flocks, which roam and rest at will,—
The distant wood, which lifts its emerald head
Towards the heavens,—the high familiar hill
(Once of the Druid Chiefs the haunt, 'tis said),— .
These tell me of my boyhood, and upbraid
My mind with passions of Youth's gushing spring,
Breathing of Hope and Love still unbetrayed
By stern experience ;—but whate'er they bring,
Alternate joy and woe, my soul shall to them cling.

There, o'er the undulating pastures fair,*
Which rise like visions of some realm of light
Within my bosom, lies the footpath where
Full oft I've trod, and, far as aching sight
Could reach into the blue, have traced the flight
Of my heart's warbler in his wanderings ;
And quaffed his spirit, fraught with wild delight,
Till I beheld earth's monarchs as but things—
Slaves to Ambition's wiles—the shepherds as true kings.

Those fields to me are as a fairy dwelling,
Haunted by innocent and lovely forms,—
The mirror of my childhood's dreams, revealing
Hopes, which have faded, but retain some charms
With sorrow blended : so the sunbeam warms
And gilds the darkling clouds on which it plays.
The flowers I loved have still their hues and balms,
The rivulet its chime, the birds their lays,
And Beauty still is here which cheered mine earlier days.

Looking abroad, scarce half a league away,
My wandering eye falls on the Haunted Lane,†
Whence walked the Lady in her white array,
And shrieked (as story tells) as if in pain,
Till Echo caught the sorrow of her strain,
And bore it onward through the shadowy night ;
And maidens, youths, and women tried in vain
To hush their fears :—they trembled with affright,
And talked with voice subdued o'er cottage fires bright.

* Sherburn Pastures.

† " The Long-Peace-Lady Lane." About fifty years ago, the
people living in the vicinity of Hallgarth, who were more superstitous

And yonder, where the curling smoke ascends
From out the valley, stands the clattering Mill.*
The murder of a gentle maiden lends,
Though long ago, a solemn memory still
Unto the spot ; whilst here the glittering rill
(Sweet though its murmers otherwise would seem)
Breathes to the ear, the tree, the vale, the hill,
The anguish of her dying groan, till stream,
And winds, and human heart, are pregnant with the theme.

There stands the dwelling of my father's friend,†
Encompassed by a growth of fine old trees
(Where noisy rooks and chattering starlings blend
Their notes on the morn and evening breeze),
And walls whose blushing cherries erst could please
My sight, and lure my boyish hands to crime.
How changed the scene ! The man who loved not ease
Has paid off Nature's debt—is done with Time,   •
And he, the wanton boy, is now in manhood's prime.

then than now, were much alarmed by cries of " murder " coming
from the direction of this lane. Tradition says that a lady was
murdered here, but when, how, and by whom, we know not; and
that her ghost frequently appeared near the spot where she had
suffered death (and had been seen by many persons), as a protest
that her blood was yet unavenged. This story was so thoroughly
believed that if some mischievous fellow who had nerve enough went
to and shouted " murder " from this lane late at night, or very early
in the morning, the pits in its immediate vicinity were laid idle for
the ensuing day : the pitmen utterly refusing to go to work, believing
that should they do so, some great calamity would befall them.

  * Hallgarth Mill, about half-a-mile to the west of the Church,
where Mary Ann Westrop was murdered by her fellow-servant,
Thomas Clark. Touching this sad event, which caused such a pain-
ful excitement throughout the North of England, and particularly
in the district where it occurred, a plain marble tablet was erected
by subscription in one of the windows of the north aisle of Pittington
Church, bearing the following inscription :—" In memory of Mary
Ann Westrop, who in the 18th year of her age, on the evening of
Sunday, the 8th of August, 1830 (during the absence of her master
and mistress), was cruelly murdered at Hallgarth Mill, in this parish,
by a man, her fellow-servant, who was executed for the offence at
Durham, on Monday, the 28th of February, 1831."

  † The residence of the late Henry Newby, Esq., an enterprising
agriculturist, who farmed Hallgarth for many years, under the
Shepherdsons.

Nearer the hallowed ground whereon I tread
With tombstones studded, verdant through Decay,
Above the trees a mansion* rears its head,
And calls up memories of another day ;
A reverend man† before me stands, and gray
With many winters, wise (evincing cares),
Humane, and humble, glowing with the ray
Religion flashes : on his brow he bears
The deep, broad stamp of Thought—his eyes are filled with tears.

Too feeble now (he prays, but weeps the while)
To pour the Spirit of his God o'er men ;
The voice, whose accents rang through every aisle,
And many hearts, I ween, and not in vain,
Is lost in sighs, nor shall return again,
For Death, the dread destroyer, lingers by :
A day and he shall know no more of pain.
Soft be his pillowed rest ! he shall not die
If Virtue, Honour, Truth, e'er blossom in the sky !

Ere yet I enter thee, old hoary pile,
Dim with the dust of ages, let me muse
A moment 'mong the tombs, while yet the smile
Of daylight shows the landscape's glorious hues.
Here sleepeth one,‡ who knew him ne'er refuse
The honour due the noble dead : his mind
Was fraught with that mild moving power, which wooes
And draws the softer passions from his kind,
Which, twined in tender cords, true friendships firmly bind.

* Hallgarth Vicarage.

† The Rev. Dr. James Miller, Vicar, who died about the year 1850.

‡ "In memory of Thomas Robinson, Sherburn, gentleman, ætat 35, obit June 28th, 1867." Mr. Robinson bravely sacrificed his life in a gallant, yet unhappily vain, attempt to rescue a drowning boy below Kepier, near Durham. Born of highly respectable parents, Mr. Robinson's education was the liberal one of a gentleman—without reference to any particular business or profession. He was first placed under the tuition of the Rev. Isaac Todd, Vicar of Shincliffe ; afterwards, at the great school of Repton, and, ultimately, with a distinguished clergyman in Derbyshire, About manhood, he studied farming with Mr. Septimus Smith, of Norham, as a useful preparation for managing his own landed property at Sherburn. But of retiring and studious habits at all times, he was perhaps more frequently within doors than without, and became, and ever

The hands, which moulder in their kindred dust,
Devoid of cunning, lost to passion's fire,
Have swept yon organ's pealing keys till burst
Sweet music's spirit forth, which e'er inspires
The breast with joy, as Jubal's heavenly lyre
Gave birth to rapture never felt before.
Enough ! since listening ears I would not tire :
Sweet be the bliss that bids his spirit soar
Through love-enchanted skies which glory's radiance pour.

Mysterious memory of one* who shined,
Perchance of Valour, in the olden time ;
Whose deeds of chivalry may have been twined
In graceful numbers and in flowing rhyme,—
Time-shrouded now, and lost, howe'er sublime.
Thy right hand grasps the sword, thy left the shield,—
Which point Imagination to thy prime,
When passion's frenzy seized thee on the field,
Where many a foeman fell ere thou to death didst yield.

afterwards continued, an ardent lover of literature—classic and
romantic—English and French—ancient and modern. One of his
accomplishments—and perhaps the dearest to him—was music. He
studied it with the greatest ardour, and attained no ordinary power
in the execution of the masterpieces of the great German and Italian
schools, both on the piano and organ. His command of the latter
instrument arose partly from early study under the celebrated
Cooper, and partly from his love of sacred music—his turn of mind,
in fact, being essentially religious. He was a lover of nature as well
as of art, and besides the noblest landscapes of our own country,
had repeatedly visited the classic beauties of Italy, and the Alpine
grandeurs of Switzerland.

* On the north side of the south aisle is the recumbent figure of a
Knight, placed here for better preservation (for he used to lie outside
the Church) by the present much and deservedly respected Vicar,
the Rev. J. Barmby. It has been suggested to us, by an undoubted
authority, that in supposing the recumbent Knight to have been a
Saxon who probably fought against the Conqueror, we appear to
have allowed our imagination too bold a flight. This view is undoubtedly correct, for the character of the armour proves him to
have been a Knight of a period considerably later than the time of
the Norman Conquest. From the bearings of the shield, so far as
we can make them out, probably he was a Lumley, or one of the
Fitz-Marmadukes, who were cognate with the Lumleys, and bore
the same arms. But nothing is known of him beyond what may be
thus conjectured.

Wast thou a leader in the ranks of death—
The Wellington of some far distant age ?
And hardy warriors, led o'er mead and heath,
Didst for the right a furious warfare wage ?
Or did Ambition's wiles thy soul engage,
And send thee onward to a goal of shame ?
Perhaps thy deeds may deck some Saxon page,
Or thou mightst win with William's host a name—
Thou answerest naught, but breathst thou honour won and fame.

The spirits of the past breathe o'er my brain,
The blue-eyed Saxon 's in my vision glassed,
Like exhumed gem, on which the light again
Shone, giving 't all the splendour of the past.
The labours of his skilful hand are cast
In ruins 'neath my feet, and, hidden, lie
A shattered wreck :—tombs, pillars, sculpture vast,
Which once in grandeur rose to greet the eye,
And charm and woo the gaze of pilgrims passing by.

There is a melancholy in the change,
Which breathes the mockery of mortal sway ;
The eye o'er vanished centuries may range,
And then behold but blossom and decay.
Thrones rise as by a magic hand to-day,
And flourish (for a little space, I ween),
Until some stronger monarch, bent on prey,
Imbued with all the fires of conquest keen,
Lays waste the halls of pride, nor weepeth o'er the scene.

And so, great Norman, in thy pride and power
Thou shiverest in his grasp a Harold's sword ;
The Saxon dynasty, this luckless hour,
Was blasted, ne'er more to be restored.
Here, Conqueror of these islands ! at thy word
These walls, uncrumbled yet, arose on high,
And stand among thy monuments abroad ;
Thy deeds are with us yet : the musing eye
Tells to the glowing mind thine immortality.

Old Church ! though vanished is thine early glory,—
The harmony of arch and column gone,
(The Modern's hand, in trying to restore thee
To former beauty, finds its skill outdone),
Thy faded frescoes now but remnants shown,—
Beyond all sacred piles I love thee yet !
'Tis not the memory of youth alone
That knits me to thee, for my cheeks are wet
From thoughts of some who sleep—I never may forget.

To the Fairy Fields of Light.

T O the fairy fields of light
      Let us go with wild delight,
        Where the fragrance of the beauty-beaming flower
          fills the air ;
      And the varied songs that flow
      From the woodlands as they blow
Will supplant the surly sorrow and dispense the dying care.

      By the rippling rills we'll rove,
      Give our choicest thoughts to love,
And pause where placid purity forms Nature's mirror there,
      And the speckled beauties glide
      Through the deep pellucid tide :
Here we'll quaff with every sense the light that leaves the
         landscape fair:

      View the sombre shade that dwells
      On the beauteous heather fells,
List the balmy zephyrs whisper with a soft æolian strain,
      Blended with the warblings wild
      Of the lark, sweet music's child,
Who pours his melting raptures o'er the pleasure-thrilling brain.

      'Tis no low ambition now
      Which wakes the bosom's glow,
In the grandeur that surrounds us shines the majesty of God,
      From the sun's refulgent light,
      And the moon and stars of night,
To the smallest ray that twinkles on the dewdrop or the flood.

In the sunset's waves of gold,
On the snowy cloudlet's fold—
A fleecy couch for Angels who would view the deeds of earth—
In the crag, the tree, the flower,
There's infinity of power,
And a splendour of construction which denotes their heavenly
birth.

Let us woo thee, lovely Sneep,*
Where the solemn shadows creep,
And the green-robed rocky ramparts rise for liberty a throne :
Here the twisting Derwent's seen,
Singing praises of the scene,
Dallying, lingering, as if loth to leave the glowing glories shone.

Now the frenzied eye may gaze,
And the soul expand with praise—
The unutterable something which we ne'er can realise :
It will not die, but burns
As the light of thought returns,
And like a rainbow blends its hues, and fades again to rise.

Here Carr† has tuned his lyre,
Whose soul thou didst inspire
With the magic of thy beauty, till he could not choose but sing :
His flowing numbers glide
In the soundings of the tide,
And are deathless as its melody, and liquid as its ring.

* To those who have not seen this beautiful natural picture which lies
on the Derwent about a mile above Allansford, a description would be
altogether vain ; and those who have not seen it would derive little benefit
from any pen and ink sketch, however well it might be drawn.

† John Carr, LL.D. of Muggleswick, author of an ode to the
Derwent, in which he speaks of the love he bore the Sneep.

John Graham Lough

But where'er the eyes repose,
In legions charms disclose,
And every sound that trembles on the ear awakes a joy :
The song-bird's warblings clear
Are softer, sweeter here,
Than those which other groves reveal, or rain adown the sky.

Strange imagination sprung,
If story be not wrong,
From the eye of genius falling on that rocky towering steep :
Lough* gazed, and lo ! arose
A " Milo " with his woes,†
And thou sharest the immortality of both, enchanting Sneep.

* John Graham Lough, the celebrated sculptor, was born at Greenhead, about a mile from the Sneep. After serving an apprenticeship as a stonemason at Shotley Field, and being engaged as a journeyman in the erection of the Newcastle Literary and Philosophical Society's Library, he betook himself to London, to push his fortune in the world of art. His journey forms one of the most romantic episodes in his life. He persuaded the captain of a collier who was just sailing for London to take him on board, offering him a guinea for his passage money, but on their arrival the captain refused to take a farthing. At Lough's request, the captain took him to the British Museum, where in company with this good, kind, rough companion, he saw what he was panting to find, the " Elgin Marbles." The captain insisted on Lough returning and sleeping on board his vessel as long as it was detained in the docks, finally urging him not to remain in such a wilderness place as London, adding, " it shall cost you nothing to go back with me to canny Newcastle." After Lough went first to London, Mr. Silvertop wished him to go to Rome to study the models of the great Italian sculptors, and offered to defray his expenses when in Rome. Lough, however, refused to go, and said that " he would not serve a second apprenticeship." Mr. Silvertop took offence at Lough's refusal to go to Rome, and left him to his unaided resources. It was, doubtless, during this period, when no hand was stretched out to help him, that he suffered the terrible privations touchingly

† It is said that Lough got his conception of " Milo " through gazing on the stupendous rocks at the Sneep. Where the association exists might puzzle a philosopher, but people of a strongly imaginative eye behold, on looking into the fire-grate, most remarkable forms—firekings, " witches skimming dizzy crags," angels, devils, mountains, chasms, valleys, &c., which to a duller eye is but a fire: as " a primrose by a river's brim " was to Peter Bell, of Wordsworth's muse, but a yellow primrose, nothing more. Alas ! for our dreams of the human family arriving at a higher state of perfection. This but describes the state of apathy into which thousands of our brothers and sisters have fallen.

> But alas ! we cannot dwell
> Always 'neath beauty's spell,—
> The curse thrown over mortals to its mission still is true :
> The evening turneth gray,
> Duty beckons us away,
> So, to all that yields us rapture, with regret, we bid adieu !

alluded to by Haydon. After a time, however, it seems that Mr. Silvertop's heart misgave him, and he called on Lough as he was engaged in his room sculpturing his Milo. Mr. Silvertop addressed him with the familiar words, "Well, Lough, how are you coming on?" Lough answered, "Oh, very well, sir ; I am working away here, and living on bread and water, as I have been accustomed to do." After this a five-pound note was sent to Lough, by or doubtless through Mr. Silvertop. While Lough was thus engaged, a circumstance occurred, which threatened to be the forerunner of his ruin, which proved, however, to be the turning point in his fortune His room being too small for the sculpturing of Milo, he could not get to the upper part of the statue so as to be able to use his chisel with sufficient freedom. What was he to do in such a case ? He acted like Alexander the Great, who cut the Gordian knot when he could not untie it. With the recklessness of a bold genius reduced to desperation, he actually broke through the ceiling of the room above him, and made for himself sufficient space to work at his statue. Hue and cry was instantly raised against him for this infraction of the rights of property. The owner began to take steps for instituting legal proceedings, and even consulted Mr. Brougham (afterwards Lord Brougham) for this purpose. Struck with the singularity of the account which was given him, Brougham went to look at the Milo, and see for himself what Lough had done. On his return from viewing Milo, Brougham told some of his friends that he had witnessed the strangest sight that ever came before him during his whole life, and narrated the circumstances. The news of the strange affair soon spread, and, before long, the whole street where Lough's room was situated was lined with the carriages of ladies and gentlemen, who had come to view the place, and to see Milo. A subscription was set on foot for Lough (to which Mr. Silvertop would doubtless contribute handsomely), the owner of the upper room was paid for the damage done to his property, and the law proceedings were staid. Lough was thus relieved from his dreadful privations, and, through orders which soon came in to him for different pieces of sculpture, the basis of his fortune was laid. The house where he modelled his Milo has been pulled down, and the spot of his early struggles and indefatigable industry is now consecrated by having a Church built on it.—*History of West Durham.*

Stanzas Written on Reading

Shelley's Poems.

IN roaming through this varied world of ours,
'Mong shadowy glens, by bubbling stream or
fountain,
Or where reflective solitude embowers,
Or tempests howl across the herbless mountain,
Or holding high communion with the flowers,
Or listening to the wild waves hollow sounding,
With what a majesty they touch the feelings,—
How chastely then the soul drinks their revealings !

Then looking on the sky, whose mighty grandeur
Defies the power of mortal mind for ever,
To comprehend how worlds on worlds do wander
Through trackless space, directed by their Giver
To an immortal goal, where not the hand or
Infinite will is seen ; then turning to the river,
Behold its glassy face glide to the ocean,
Say dost thy soul not thrill with deep emotion ?

Look on the leaves which come not till the season
Of genial Spring, whose mild rains steep the earth,
And call the flow'rets from their ice-bound prison
In blushing fragrance to their annual birth.
Then Summer comes like thing endowed with reason,
And draws the blue snake from his dark cave forth ;
Then Autumn reaps the harvest of the sun,
Completing what her sister Spring begun.

The Nightingale to night and solitude
Pours out his soul, which trembles over earth ;
The laverock, from his watch-tower in the cloud
His flowing thrilling song of praise sends forth ;
The blackbird, piping in the echoing wood,
The thrush and linnets warbling, give birth
To soft and tender passion, and are fraught
With food for wildest, sweetest, dearest thought.

" The golden glowworm in her dewy dell,"
The insect tribe of many a beauteous hue,
Which charm the eye and bid the bosom swell,
The twinkling brilliance of a drop of dew,
The bow of heaven which strikes us like a spell,
And all the harmony of things, not few,
Are but the breathings of the Deity,
To wake the slumbering soul to prospects in the sky.

The painted Indian, God's untutored child,
Whose savage orbs ne'er gazed upon a book,
Save the wide volume of his native wild,—
The mountain, forest, lake, and whispering brook,—
Heaven's azure dome, whose million meek eyes smiled,
And seemed the spirit of them all to look
Into his soul, which knew no other law
Than that by nature taught, inspiring awe,—

The lofty hills in hoary majesty,—
The rippling brooklet and the murmuring waves,—
The fragrant airs which through the valley sigh
The trees, the flowery plains, and echoing caves,—
The lightning's flash along the gloomy sky,—
The roaring thunders when the storm-king raves,—
Have writ their language on his willing soul,
And prove th' " Great Spirit" author of the whole.

Then, Shelley, thou would'st tell us " there's no God,"
All Nature gives thy impious words the lie ;
If, sooth, thou sufferedst from His chastening rod,
And failing to detect with erring eye
The object of the ruling hand abroad,
Which sweeps the desert, ocean, and the sky,
Had'st thou no remedy, but darkly mope
And vainly try to blight our happiness and hope ?

Think'st thou, vain man, because endowed with thought
To make the lightning serve thy mighty will
And chainless intellect, that thou art fraught
With power Omnipotent ?   That matchless skill
Of deeds immortal sprang by chance from nought ?
That thy transcendent strength to save or kill
Had no more worthy origin ?   Go, bow
Before yon mossy rock, 't has greater faith than thou.

Immortal Shelley ! thou whose mental might
Played with ideas, as with toys a child,
Rocks, mountains, rivers, oceans, skies, thy light
Shone on them as the lightning's flash ; though wild
Thy fevered brain could feel, impart delight,
Enchanting man ; then thou hast turned and smiled,
And from thy faithless heart exclaimed, " no God
Reigns over us ; " hence Chance inspired a clod !

There is a God ! and on Him man will lean
And build his storied hopes while dwelling here,
Wearing, from solace, that meek, gentle mien,
That speechless eloquence of silenced fear,
No dread of death such aspect bears ; serene
And calm, as lovely waveless lakes appear,
The heavens reflected in their depths below
In starry beauty's quiet slumber glow.

There is a glory in Religious teaching
Inspired with bliss and joy, no tongue can tell ;
Nor Atheist's laugh, nor Deist's soulless preaching
Can break the magic of the sacred spell,
Where Faith and Hope like sirens sing, bewitching
The heart, where darkling sorrows wont to dwell,
Begetting Love and Peace, the aim of Him
Before whose eyes all their lights are dim.

Say, Shelley, wast thou happy here below ?
Did not the passion in thy bosom nursed,
Become to thee to all mankind a foe,
And leave thee, e'en in youth, a thing accursed ?
Did'st never see the Christian's face a-glow
With tranquil smiles, or hear the heavenly burst
Of music from his joy o'erburthened breast,
Which marked his future home, a home of rest ?

Whate'er has Atheism done for this our world
But curse it ?   Has Paine's infidelity
Not many a million to destruction hurled,
By the sad aid of heartless Sophistry ?
The sails which bore his bark of life were furled
O'er awful, writhing, helpless agony !
Contrast his death with Addison's, and see
The calm that waits on Christianity.

Vain, godless man hath tried, but never yet
Left e'en one record on historic page
Which breathes felicity.   Men may forget,
And have, in this and every other age,
Their living God ; but ne'er or seldom set,
(When future glory would the soul engage)
Their hopes on aught short of the mighty Rock
Which stands the tempests breath and earthquake's shock.

Oh ! misery, nursed of hate, about the heart
Entwines, as snakes around their victims bound,
Till man becomes a fiend from poison's smart,
Yet planted there the immedicable wound,
Cherishing wretchedness with miser art,
Till Sin has left him in a gulf profound,
Companion to Despair, and ceaseless pain,
Where radiant hope may never beam again.

Our chance is all with virtue.   Our despair
Springs out of Vice's most detested fruit ;
If nought beyond the grave could claim our care,
And blotted from our souls each, every doubt,
Nothing to dread more than our sufferings here,
And death were final when our breath goes out,
Still let me with Religion, Virtue dwell,
And shun thy spirit, Vice, which makes fair earth a hell.

Lines to the Derwent.

IF, Derwent, in his dearth of power,
  An humble votary sing thy praise
In weaker strains than whom thy dower
  Of loveliness inspired to pour
Their loftier, sweeter lays,

Chide not ; he loves as well as they
Who quaffed thy changing seasons' charms,
When rocks were rent and borne away
As feathers 'neath thy wanton spray,
  In frowning grandeur's arms :

Or milder Spring, whose genial gale
Had soothed thy mane—adorned thy braes,
Or Summer spread her deeper veil,
Or hoary Autumn did reveal
  Her glory-tinted face.

How sweet thy sylvan shades to rove,
Or on thy sunny banks to lie ;
To list the blending lays of love,
That gush from every echoing grove,
Or rain adown the sky ;—

To catch the glow of beauty's face,
And ponder well each floweret's eye :
To dwell upon its peerless grace,
Its birth in Nature's God to trace,
To thrill with wakened joy ;—

To look on heaven-aspiring trees,
Adorned in vernal robes of green ;
Their graceful motions as the breeze
Embraces each, till like the seas
Their heaving breasts are seen ;—

To muse within the silent dell,
While resting on some mossy stone
(Where Nature's shadowy glories dwell),
On fern and herb, and floral bell,
Enraptured and alone ;—

To trace thee to the infant rills,*
When summer's tints enchant the eye,
That gush between the purple hills,
Where hums the bee—the laverock trills
His melting melody ;—

---

* The source of the Derwent, about a mile and a half above Blanchland, is well worth a visit. At the confluence of two small streams which have their fountains among the wild, yet beautiful, heather hills, stands a remarkable rock known by the formidable name of "Gibraltar." Beneath the brow of this romantic pile, which occupies the narrow neck of land formed by those burns, and towards the junction of the same, is to be seen a bright spring well, which will gladden the heart of the visitor. The woods on either side from this spot to Bay Bridge (about a mile), in the valley of the Derwent, are positively charming to those who have an eye for the majesty of Nature.

To linger by the hoary-rocks
Which guard as sentinels thy way,
Crowned with the hardy heather's locks,
Braving the strong-wing'd tempests' shocks,
Or lit with summer's ray ;—

To watch thy tributaries roll
In soft and soothing light along ;
To hear their bells of liquid toll,
Or prattle as some mystic soul
Their waters dwelt among ;—

To mount some promontory's height,
Commanding well thy winding ways,
And turn the eye in wild delight
Upon thy margin's fringes bright,
Knoll, woodland, glen and field, where light
And beauty mingled blaze !

Yes, Derwent, 'tis no meagre joy
That thrills their hearts who roam thy shore :
I loved thee when a trembling boy,
For thou hast wondrous charms ; my eye
Beholds but to adore.

As on some bright enchanted stream,
By fairies trod I dreamt of thee :
Thou wert my bosom's earliest theme
Ere it was wont on rhymes to dream,
But fetterless and free.

Nor is this strange ; for she to whom
I owe my being—all I know
Of thoughts which out of virtue come—
Was reared, and wore her maiden bloom
Upon thy banks,—drank their perfume
And music of thy flow.

My bosom long has been the shrine—
A cherished sanctuary—where
Her stories superstitous twine,
And blend with visions more divine
Committed to my care.

Say, Derwent, thou who art so old,
Thou can'st, if that thou wilt, I think,
Strange stories of the past unfold
Of nature's savage child who strolled
First on thy sounding brink.

Thou'st seen him 'neath the Roman's spear
Sink trembling on the flowery sod,
And heard him with distracted ear
His deities invoking there ;
For oh ! he knew not God.

Tell me, has many a Saxon maid,
Of flaxen lock and azure eye,
Thy stilly wave a mirror made,
And, lingering, her bright face surveyed
Of blushing roses dye ?

Thou must, if tales be true, have felt
The trip of gentle Ebba's* feet,
And heard her as by thee she knelt,
Her soul to adoration melt,
In accents wild and sweet.

The Christian's God, for she had known
The " Prince of Peace," inspired her prayer ;
With face upturned towards His throne,
To solitude and thee alone
Of earth she told her care.

* For an account of St. Ebba, see page 59.

Say, Derwent, do her ashes rest
In some deep glen or mound of thine?
'Tis sad that o'er so pure a breast
No monumental marks attest
To human eye the worthy guest
That fills so dear a shrine.

Thou must have checked thy crystal tide
When erst the impious Dane appeared,
And wrapped in flames the house of pride,
Which rose in splendour on thy side,
This royal maiden reared :

Or frowned as through thy bosom rushed
The host* from Caledonia wild ;
Thy hoarser sounds to silence hushed,
As Ethelberga† gazing blushed,
For she was virtue's child.

Had Edwin or Paulinus‡ tuned
To sing thy praises no 'rapturing lyre?
Did Radcliffe's§ generous bosom bound,
When first thy hallowed charms he found,
And burn with po'tic fire ?

* The Scotch, 30,000 strong, led by David II, King of Scotland,
crossed the Derwent at Ebchester, after traversing some miles of the
Roman Road, "Watling Street," and encamped at night amid the ruins
of the Vindomora of the Itinerary of Antoninus, before proceeding to
the battle of Neville's Cross, which terminated so disastrously for the
brave Scots. The King fell into the hands of the English, and was kept
in captivity eleven years.

† Ethelberga, the wife of King Edwin, who succeeded Ethelfred, and
reigned from 626 to 633 over Northumbria.

‡ Paulinus, Archbishop of York, a Roman missionary, who came
north with King Edwin and Ethelberga in 626, converted thousands
of Northumbrian Britons, and Edwin himself to christianity ; and when
Edwin fell in the battle of Hatfield Chase, in Yorkshire, fled with the
royal widow and her children, and found an asylum in Kent.

§ See page 62.

Did classic Carr* once converse hold
With Lucian in thy tranquil bowers,
Until the lengthening shadows told
How far the western sun had rolled
Adown the fruitful hours ?

The Briton loved thy oaken shade ;
The Roman built his temple here ;
The Saxon shook his conquering blade ;
The desolating Dane surveyed
The piles he did not spare.

Upon thy banks the Norman reared
His abbey gray,† devotion's home ;
And those whom Luther's creed revered
Nestled within thy breast, nor feared
The Christian martyr's doom.

Thou answerest nought.   Thy secrets keep
The centuries have given :
Still on to father ocean sweep
Thy chainless tides, and sing and weep
And purl and roar to Heaven !

* See page 32.

† " The Abbey of Blanchland, or Alba Landa, was founded in 1175 by
Walter de Bolbeck.   It was forfeited to the crown by the attainder of
Thomas Forster, jun., Esq., 1715, and purchased by the Right Honourable
and Rev. Lord Crewe, Bishop of Durham, his uncle, who left it to
charitable uses.   The west end and towers of the church remain.   There
are some old gravecovers in the church.   The gateway of the quadrangle
of the abbey, and of the abbey itself, are still remaining ; the towers on
each hand are converted into alehouses ; but there remain no relics of
the impressive church pomp of former times."

The Lost Hunter; or, an Incident of Life in Illinois.

HE passed the gate ere the storm came on,
  Which led to the dreary wild ;
I marked him well : he was all alone,
With a gun across his shoulder thrown,
  And an aspect brave and mild.

"Stranger," I said, in a voice of fear,
  (Breathing a timely warning),
"Thou must not 'tempt the prairie drear ;
The way is long, and night is here,
  And thou might'st be lost ere morning."

And he paused and spake in gentle mood,.
  For the brave are always kind :
"From youth, my boy, I have tempests wooed,
On the open plain, in the shrieking wood,
  As it groaned 'neath the rushing wind."

So onward he passed in his active might,
   As a steed freed from the rein,
Over the crests of the snow-wreathes white,
Till he seemed but a speck in my aching sight,
   On the far extending plain.

But, hark ! how the storm-king wails on high,
   With his thousand voices moaning,
Pregnant with many a destiny ;
And the forest trees, as he passes by,
   Beneath his rage are groaning.

And the snow is borne on the warring blast,
   As a mist the land enshrouding ;
Oh ! where is the bold one who lately passed ?
Will he brave the storm, or be over-cast,
   O'er his reckless folly brooding ?

By far Sangamon's tideless stream,
   In a cottage lone and drear,
A woman sits by her log-fire's gleam,
   And her brain is wrought with foreboding fear
As she hears the wind go whistling on,
And the oaks around 'neath its pressure groan,
And the oxen low in the frozen shed,
And the restless grunt of the hog in his bed,
And the horse's neigh, and the dog's low growl,
As he hears the wolf's long echoing howl,
And the awful night-bird piping loud,
Like a spirit pent in a sable cloud.
'Tis an evil omen : all presume
That some much-loved friend has found a tomb.
To her, all things wear sorrow's form ;—
   Despair is written on her brow,
And she turns to gaze through the blinding storm,
   With an eye almost prophetic now ;
And from the depths of her welling woes,
This impassioned song of sorrow flows :—

" Where does my loved one stray from me ?
　He never stayed so long before ;
A day were an eternity
　Should he no longer cross my door.

" My fondest hope—my life—my all,
　Since first I gazed upon his face ;
If love for me has wrought his fall,
　Why died I not in his embrace ?

" But, no ! he would not leave the grove
　In such a wild tempestuous hour ;
Perchance some foe to mortal love
　Has clasped him in his giant power.

" And yet, O God ! he never dwelt
　A night beyond my tender care, ·
Since first we at the altar knelt,
　Our souls for ever mingling there.

" He yet may come ; away despair !
　Why seek a home within my breast ?
Thou never sought'st a heart to cheer ;
　Thou foe to hope, devouring rest.

" But if he sleeps beneath the snow,
　My woes shall only end in death ;
Then blow, relentless tempests, blow,
　And chill for e'er my vital breath."

　　　*　　　*　　　*　　　*　　　*

'Tis Spring ; the zephyrs sweep across the plain,
    And flowers of varied hues are breathing here,
And Love, and Light, and Beauty smile again,
    In the enchantment of the youthful year.

The wild deer strays in grace and majesty,
    " Brushing the morn and evening dews away,"
Cropping the early swamp grass eagerly,
    Or basking 'neath the enamouring god of Day.

And man, the base destroyer, seeks thy bed,
    To slay thee through some cunning he has plann'd ;
Or sends thee panting with his fiery steed,
    To die at length beneath his cruel hand.

In such a chase, when low his victim lay,
    .A hunter had descended from his horse,
To drive the last breath from the prostrate clay,
    In boasted triumph rather than remorse.

This done, he turned his eye abroad to learn
    If any of his comrades wandered near ;
Some stranger object did his eye discern,
    Which he approached with something like to fear.

Some whitened bones—a skeleton—a man—
    A gun—some rags of him who passed the gate,
" O ! noble Tom," his sorrows then began,
    ." As I do live, the world shall know thy fate.

" And was it here, by awful foes surrounded,
    The elements which froze thy vital tide,
And wolves which thou so often hast confounded,
    Thou droopedst in agony and bravely died ?

                                    F.

" Thy very bones have suffered from fierce fangs,
   Which tore the flesh in savage hunger here ;
O, what ! ere life had fled, would be thy pangs ;
   Here rests the theme of many a ' generous tear.'

" Thou shalt not linger in the scorching sun,
   Where eyes of reverence may never stray ;
Near thy loved cot, now tenantless and lone,
   Where Sangamon rolls slowly on her way,

" Thou shalt repose in an eternal sleep,
   Where fairer flowers than these shall deck thy bed,
And willows, gemmed with morning dew, shall weep
   Their glittering tears above thy lowly head.

My story's done ; but where, O ! where is she
   Who pour'd her sorrow's to the midnight skies—
Where Sangamon glides slow and noiselessly
   Below the banks where sturdy white oaks rise ?

Gone with the spirit she so much adored ;
   Their bones are mingling in one quiet grave ;
This epitaph was to their memory pour'd :—
   " Here lie the relics of the True and Brave."

"Yon sacred pile its sombre head uprears."

Ebchester Church in the Olden Time.

Ebchester.*

ERE let me sit upon these grassy slopes,
Beneath the god of Day's enamouring beam,
Enchanted with the scene which round me opes,
Prolific text of many a cherished dream,
Whose blooming landscapes with chaste beauties teem :
The smiling field, the glen, the burn, the grove,
Blending harmoniously around thy stream,
Meandering Derwent, fit retreat for Love,
Where Nature's worshipper in joy unmixed may rove.

* Few places in the county possess a greater charm for the historian
than the village of Ebchester, whose early history is shrouded in
obscurity, and whose unique Church and Roman relics have long
employed the thoughts of reflecting and speculative antiquaries.
The Roman legions who made it their resting place, and from the
sloping banks watched the tactics of the hardy Briton concealed in
the opposite forests of Northumbria, the callous Dane, and defiant,
unconquerable Scot, all have left upon it the impress of their strength
and power.   Pleasantly situated on the right bank of the Derwent,
and intersected by the road leading from Newcastle to Shotley
Bridge, at a distance of twelve miles from the former and two from
the latter, the village has undergone little change since Hutchinson's
time.   It was then a small, irregular place, and the description holds
good at the present day.   Notwithstanding the modern hotel, and
two or three pretentious grocery and drapery establishments, an air
of rustic simplicity still hangs over it. ' Scarcely two of the houses
are alike, one jutting upon and another receding from the street, and
most of them seemingly built from the readily available quarry
adjacent—the Roman Station.   Very little is known respecting the
early history of the Church, which stands within the area of the
Roman Camp, and is dedicated to St. Ebba.   It is built of stones
from the Roman walls and edifices, and apparently dates from the
twelfth century.   The engraving correctly depicts the Church as it
was before being restored, and presents a curious combination of
early and modern architecture.—*History of West Durham.*

My mind contemplative through mists of Time,
On Retrospection's airy pinions borne,
Beholds, where now those towering woods sublime,
Aspiring to the clouds, the hills adorn,
The heathen Briton who had yet to learn
A Roman's majesty or Saxon's will,
Roaming those haunts, in savage gloom forlorn,
Through dell and grove, or pausing by the rill,
In which he saw no God, but worshipped Idols still.

He hears the voices of the gale—the woods,
The liquid bells, where murmuring brooks meander,
The tempest's shriek along the sable clouds,
The echoing cavern and the roaring thunder,
Sees lightnings flash—the sky's transcendent grandeur,
Lists feathery choirs their melting music fling
Unto the winds, and forth he thus doth wander,
Snuffing the floweret's fragrance—lovely thing,
Yet dreams not of their Source from whence all glories spring.

And in my gaze I see the Druid chief
Beneath the oak he venerates at prayer,
Or in rude temple pouring strange belief
To Deity more strange, or false god there ;
And mark the " wicker cage " around Despair,
The howling victims wreathed in torturing flame ;
The clouds are red with the unholy glare,
And cruel wretches, never known to shame,
Survey with fierce delight what Hell would fail to name.

Now turn we to our antiquated theme,
Ebchester : I have roamed from thee afar.
Here lordly Romans dwelt with power supreme,
In all the pomp and pageantry of war ;
Here frowned their rampart wall, a massy bar,
To British hosts impregnable, I ween ;
And where these tranquil habitations are,
Whose happy inmates smile in joys serene,
Unshocked by din of arms, nor caring what has been,

The towering temple rose, where mirth and revelry
Basked in the rays of Triumph and of Power ;
The song, the jest, the tale of chivalry,
Beguiled, no doubt, full many a flying hour.
Here, Antoninus,* thou whose earthly dower,
In Hadrian's gift, was Rome's imperial throne,
Was reared thy " Vindomora "—now no more,
Like to thy virtuous self—thy Empire—gone ;
Yet Rome, thy glory, still smiles round us as a sun !

The air and earth are pregnant with thy prime,
Immortal Roman ; and man looks on thee
As a Colossus, towering up through time,
Or a lone Alp, soaring majestic'ly,
Which grows more mighty as he longingly
Turns and returns, as if each glance he cast
Some greater wonder left his breast less free,
Till it becomes a thing so huge and vast,
That all the world beside seems utterly surpassed.

* The author has designedly preferred the character of Antoninus
Pius the Sixteenth, in order of the Roman Emperors from Julius
Cæsar, to that of Antoninus, the author of an Itinerary (or military
road book), on whose authority, coupled with that of Richard of
Cirencester, modern writers believe the Station at Ebchester to be
the Vindomora of the Romans.   In an excellent paper on Roman
Ebchester, contributed to the " History of West Durham" by the Rev.
Dr. Hooppell, Rector of Byers Green, the writer says :—" There can
be no doubt the Romans, in giving names to their military stations
in Britain, adopted the enchorial, that is the native, names of the
places.   All they did was to affix, in the generality of cases, a Latin
termination to the word, so as to fit it to receive the various inflections
the nature of their language required, and, in some cases, to soften
the harshness, or remove the unpronounceability by their lips, of
the gutterals.   Thus the signification of the name Vindomora, the
Roman name of Ebchester, must be sought in the Keltic, *i.e.*, in the
British, language.   Nor is it hard to discover.   ' Vin' signifies, in
the British, ' Edge,' and occurs in numerous instances.   Vinovium,
Vindobala, Vindogladia, Vindolana, are all found in Roman lists of
posts in Britain.   ' Do' seems certainly to be the Latinised form of
' Du' Black, and ' Mor' is the same word that we have in our
language still, written with a doubled ' o'—Moor.   Vindomoro is,
therefore, ' Black moor edge,'—a name, probably, in British times,
remarkably descriptive of the position and vicinity of the spot now
known as Ebchester."

Tradition tells, and I repeat the story,
That 'neath this village, in some cave, was hid,
When Rome had boundless wealth and too had glory,
A chest of money, and upon its lid
A crow was perched, and some old man to rid
His brain (whose nightly dreams oppressed him sore)
Of doubt regarding what the Romans did,
Worked hard for weeks the treasure to explore,
But neither gold nor crow to light could e'er restore.*

Deem not, because the old man dug in vain,
That nought of Rome hath hither been exhumed ;
The bath, the altar,† and inscription plain
Of mortals, who below had been entombed
Eight hundred years, ere Norman foes presumed
To wave their sceptre o'er this sea-girt isle,
Have been extractèd from this soil, long doomed
To lie like graves in dungeons, where no smile
Of summer sunb'eam came to light and cheer the while.

About this hallow'd spot a charm seems hov'ring ;
The fragmentary ruins here we find,
Divested by some busy hand of cov'ring,
Are eloquent of man's immortal mind,
And are with Roman genius entwined;
As ivy clambers o'er the mouldering wall,
With vigour in its wreck-surviving rind,
So Thought outlives its flesh-encumbering hall,
And walks the earth with Time triumphant over all.

* Tradition says that a chest of Roman money is buried somewhere in the Station, and that a crow is perched on its lid. About fifty years ago, an old man, who profoundly believed the story, set to work and sunk, in different parts of Ebchester, two shafts, where he laboured with a will some weeks, in the hope of finding the treasure, but success did not crown his efforts. He finally abandoned the work, more through exhaustion than failing faith in the money being buried somewhere within the precincts of the old Station.

† The Church and Churchyard abound in Roman sculptures, which are fully described in the *History of West Durham*. Close to the entrance to the Church, just outside the porch, on its western side, is a noble altar. (See illustration on the next page). It was found in the year 1876, at the last restoration of the Church, in the foundations at the west end.

Roman Altar found in 1876.

Whence emanates the petty pride of man ?
Great Cæsar and Agricola are clay,
Brave Hadrian and Antoninus ran
A course of glory, but have passed away,—
Their mem'ries o'er our hearts like sunbeams play.
Come hither, mortal, and survey this spot ;
Mark well the scene of power and grandeur's stay ;
What is it now ?   Such soon shall be thy lot,
Save that thy very name, perchance, will be forgot.

Fair, gentle, chaste, and beauteous Ebba,* thou
(Long, long ago, twelve hundred changeful years)
Didst cause a Monastery to rise, where now
Yon sacred pile its sombre head uprears ;
Here, in seclusion, didst thou dwell, with fears
Lest worldly passions should corrupt thy breast,
Nursing thy virtue in this vale of tears
With Christian watchfulness which sought not rest
But in His bosom, who had made thine own more blest.

Perchance Paulinus,† he whose skilful tongue,
Converting kings, was eloquent of Truth,
Had sought thee, Ebba, first of Christians wrung
From royal pleasures and their sins forsooth,
And kept thee strong in Faith, though still in youth,
Beneath his vigilant and heaven-rayed eye,
Beholding virtues in their tender growth
Developing to fit thee for the sky,
But dreamt not of thy fate, thy future agony.

* St. Ebba, daughter of King Ethelfrid, who reigned over Northumbria from 593 to 617, is said to have founded a Monastery here in, or before, the year A.D. 660. It is also said that after the destruction of the Monastery, St. Ebba and her virgins disfigured their faces to save themselves from the impious Danes. St. Ebba was amongst the first Royal Christians.

† Paulinus, Archbishop of York, was an Italian by birth, and is thought to have taken monastic vows in the Monastery of St. Andrew's, in Rome, in 601. He was sent to England by Gregory the Great, as an adjunct of the missionaries there—Augustin and his companions. Paulinus afterwards, on the marriage of King Edwin of Kent to Ethelburga, accompanied the Christian Princess to the north when Edwin ascended the Northumbrian throne. Edwin, under the preaching of Paulinus, was induced to espouse the Christian faith, and thousands of Northumbrian Britons as well.

'Thy royal father's daughter had her sorrows
In this dark voyage of ever-varying strife ;
Thy cruel sire* but knew the joy that borrows
Existence from a foeman robbed of life ;
The slayer of the Briton's soul was rife
With hell's dark passions deepening their stain,
Till Death approached him with his certain knife,
As if to urge in justice pain for pain,
And laid him pulseless down, the slayer with the slain.

And did he fall unwept of mortal eyes ?
Methinks, fair Ebba, that some kindred soul
Poured forth its sorrows to the midnight skies,
The wailing griefs which it might ne'er control,
That mixed with rocky Derwent's echoing roll,
Till lost in air as boundless as its woe ;
And shall they find at length some distant goal,
Or live and sigh in all the winds that blow,
And visit every clime ?   We know nought—even so !

Ebba, thy life 'neath this monastic roof
No doubt had something of a latent charm ;
Thou deemed'st its massy walls were tempest proof
To shield thyself and cherished ones from harm :
Thy dream was vain ; Northumbria's land was warm
With blazing temples, palaces and fanes,
Like to the Simoon or the thunder storm,
They came ! they came ! the hope-devouring Danes,
And wrapped thy home in fire, rewarding thus thy pains.

---

* The cruelties of Ethelfrid (who, we are informed, destroyed more Britons than all the other Saxon kings), are well known to those who are acquainted with our Anglo-Saxon history. Who has not read with horror of his slaughter of 1,200 unresisting Britons at Bangor, the destruction of the ancient monastery there—its vast library, the collection of ages, the repository of the most precious monuments of the ancient Britons, &c. ? Ethelfrid fell on the banks of the Idel, in Nottinghamshire, in battle against Redwald.

And there the pile thy dearest thought had cherished,
Lay smouldering o'er the spirit of thy bliss,
Thy tenderest hopes of earthly glory perished,
Expiring on the red flame's crackling hiss :
But ere, alas ! thy fortune came to this,
Thou fled'st in terror like a timid deer,
Oe'r vale and plain and craggy precipice,
Imploring heaven thy drooping soul to cheer,
And save thee from the Danes—those' impious lords of fear.

Then ancient Coldingham thy home became,
Where lived the classic Bede in after time,
The gifted Saxon of enduring fame,
The modest genius of lore sublime :
Here, Ebba, still the memory of crime
Pursued the Abbess of this holy place :
The heartless Dane, who spared not virtue's prime,
In dread of whom thou galled'st thy comely face,
Can't now defile thy dust, which never knew disgrace.

Strange ends has wanton Desolation* wrought ;
Behold where splendour girt by Power did dwell,
And mighty Rome the hardy Briton fought,
The lonely Hermit seeks his quiet cell
'Mid Vindomora's ruins, bound to quell
The world within him which his soul abhors :
A waste extends, the sheltering woodlands tell
Of safety—an orison he pours,
And to the vaults of heaven Imagination soars.

He quaffs the sheeny rill like star-beams sparkling,
Whose placid waters are his only mirror.;
With Peace he wanders by the forest darkling,
For Solitude for him has got no terror ;
His breast is calm and pure, no worldly sorrow
Distracts the pilgrim of this sylvan scene ;
If life has nought of ecstasy, no horror
Death can have : he waits with brow serene
The stroke which kings approach with pale and trembling mien.

* Five or six centuries after the destruction of the Monastery, we
find hermits nestling in the ruins of Vindomora.

On yonder bank washed by this rippling river,
(Soft sympathy directs my tearful eye
To him whose fate e'en blighting Time shall never
Brush from the tablets of man's memory),
Brave Radcliffe !* part of thy possessions lie :
The hand that clothed the orphan, fed the poor,
And checked the sorrow of the widow's sigh,
Reclines in dust, and shall relieve no more,
While England's honoured sons thy hapless end deplore.

Thy ancient hall has crumbled stone by stone ;
Now but in fragments are its ruins found,
The mantling ivy's emerald tresses thrown,
Have wrapped those more than hallowed relics round
In amorous embrace, as if 'twere bound
To save them from the revels of decay :
Here silence reigns unbroken by a sound,
Save when some songbird from the trembling spray
Pours forth his tender notes in soul-enrapturing lay.

Lamented Radcliffe ! ill thy beauteous face,
Thy open hand where want could be supplied,
Thy form whose symmetry breathed angel grace,
Where all the virtues dwelt in glowing pride,
Were spared by those who reverenced thee, and vied
In their unrivalled love for thee and thine :
Though thou hast fought by foul Rebellion's side,
Though streaks of indiscretion blot thy line,
Thy "name smells sweet of Heaven"—there may thy soul,
　　　　too, shine.

" Thy creed has been thy curse," some spirits sing,
At least so far as earthly prospects go :
Alas ! it is a strange and awful thing
That men's opinions should work such woe :
Our choice of ways to heaven makes many a foe
'Mong those denying charity a home,
Whose bosoms never wake the thoughts which glow,
But nurse, like narrow cells, the midnight gloom,
Where Love and Light are not, and Pity finds no room.

* Radcliffe.—James, third Earl of Derwentwater, who owned land
on the left bank of the Derwent, whose misfortunes are too well known
to need further notice here.

Then shall these passions pall our joys for ever,
And send us darkling on our devious road,
Like the mad torrents of a mighty river,
Whose vengeful waters have its banks o'erflowed ?
No ! let us hope : behold a change abroad.
The Truth shall triumph, Love shall yet be king,
And rid the earth of Hate, encumbering load,
That erst did mar and blight affection's spring,
And reign supreme o'er earth and bliss to mortals bring.

Here, where the skin-clad painted Briton roved,
The Roman triumphed, and the Saxon reigned,
The callous plundering Dane beheld unmoved
The bleeding heart his passion had profaned,
The Norman trod when Saxon strength had waned,
Peace, lovely Peace ! is monarch of the spot,
And Happiness, of none but fools disdained,
Pervades the air, the castle, and the cot,
And Virtue's lovely face is fair, without a blot.

This tranquil village basks in heaven's smile ;
On hills surrounding lordly mansions rise,
The brooklet purling to the flowers the while ;
The far celestial laverock's melodies
Rain on the ear like angel's symphonies :
The backbird's song and Derwent's dashing roar,
Mingling with mother Nature's thousand sighs,
Fall on the brain with power unfelt before,
To crush the meaner thoughts and bid the nobler soar.

O dove-eyed Peace ! how comely are thy ways,
Impregnate with the spirit of thy sire ;
Who knows thee best is worthiest of praise,
For ne'er within him burns unhallowed fire,
But harps attuned by Virtue's siren choir
Across his breast their soothing murmurs fling ;
O Peace ! long may the minstrel wake his lyre
The merits of thy happy reign to sing,
But give the highest praise to Heaven's Eternal King.

Stanzas in Memory of Dr. Renton.*

DEATH ! how doubly cruel was thine arrow
That laid our generous friend for ever low,
To lie oblivious in a cavern narrow,
Where neither love, nor hope, nor light may glow,
Nor sunbeam stray, nor soft-winged zephyrs blow ;
But rest may come at length in calm repose.
The poor have lost a friend, and vice a foe,
And all a lofty spirit, which arose
Like to a star which sheds a radiance while it glows.

* John Renton, Esq., of Orchard House, Shotley Bridge, long
and popularly known as Dr. Renton, was born in Edinburgh on the
12th February, 1812, and was educated at the High School and also
at the University of his native city. After finishing his curriculum,
he was engaged as assistant to Dr. Lowrey, of Corbridge, when he
began to manifest those sterling qualities, not the least of which was
an unbending moral rectitude, which so strongly characterised his
after life. While yet a young man, Mr. Renton began practising

He lived not for himself; he never knew
A thought which would disgrace the noblest mind.
Intelligence was stamped upon his brow,
Where stern, yet tender, passions were enshrined ;
A spirit always brave and ever kind,
Which threw the magic of its spell o'er men,—
An airy fetter out of virtues twined,—
That drew them round him as he would, and when
They most of reverence felt he turned to earth again.

He sank to earth amid the sorrowing tears
Of those who knew him best, hence loved him most,
With honours gathered from the rolling years,
And virtues that e'en monarchs may not boast.
They shall not be on erring mortals lost ;
Mankind will nurse, as hope, his memory,
While on life's changing, billowy ocean tossed,
And breathe its glowing lessons to the free,
Till " work and persevere " the worthy motto be.

on his own account in the little village of Slaley, but his sagacious
judgment soon fixed upon Shotley Bridge as a locality better cal-
culated for the development of his plans of future effort, and subsequent events proved he was not mistaken. His practice gradually
increased, work seemed to be his natural element, and his dispensing
establishment at Slaley, which was carried on for some years after
his removal to Shotley, received the most unremitting attention.
Shortly after his establishment at Shotley Bridge, he had the good
fortune to be appointed medical attendant to the Silvertop family,
and so satisfied was Mr. Silvertop with the medical treatment he
received, that at his death he bequeathed Dr. Renton one hundred
guineas over and above the payment of his bill. Such a generous
appreciation as this of the professional talent of Dr. Renton tended
in no limited degree to establish him in popular estimation. About
1854, he was appointed medical superintendent to the Consett Iron
Company's workmen, which appointment he held till his death on
February 18th, 1870. In matters pertaining to the well-being of the
locality in which he was placed, Dr. Renton was ever foremost. He
was one of the chief promoters of the first agricultural society in the
district, and was its chairman during the period of its existence.
He was also one of the first to establish the Horticultural Society,
contributing largely for its support in its infancy, and justly proud

F

Thus in our bosoms shall he still live on,
Nor thought nor deed of his shall pass away;
Mind walks the earth with Time, and he had one
Fraught with the lustre of refulgent day:
Our children's children may be heard to say—
" His hand was open, as his heart was true,
" He sought heaven's gracious bounty to repay
" Through charity, for he was one of few
" Who live and work, that they at length some good may do."

of its growing proportions.   Dr. Renton was likewise one of the
management committee for the establishment of the Gas Company,
and was for many years chairman of the board of directors; indeed,
in everything connected with the prosperity of the district, he was a
prominent and painstaking supporter.

Tom Lough.[*]

I SING no slave to Luxury and Pride ;
  An humble Poet-Artist is my theme,
Whom Folly's thoughtless slaves do e'er deride,
  Through lacking knowledge of the heavenly dream
Which sweeps his bosom as a tameless tide,
  Awak'ning thoughts that as a torrent team,
As Inspiration drives his glowing pen,
Where Folly feels the lash, and writhes again.

---

* Tom Lough was born at Greenhead, three miles west of Shotley
Bridge, at the commencement of this century. His parents afterwards
removed to Muggleswick with their family, where Tom would get his
first education in reading, writing and arithmetic ; and learned from the
romantic scenery around him, "to look on Nature with a poet's eye,"
to tune his violin to the voices of the songbirds, the sighs of the summer
gales, and the wails, the shrieks, and roars of the winter tempests. His
imitation of the voices of the latter season would, I have no doubt, be
the most perfect. It was here that the late learned George Silvertop,
Esq., of Minsteracres, found Tom and his brother John in their father's
cottage, plying their artistic talents. According to Haydon, the celebrated painter, when Mr. Silvertop entered the cottage he found the
ceilings and walls all drawn over, and models of human limbs and arms
in clay lying about in all directions. Pope's Homer and a volume of

Robed in no colours gay of blushing hue,
   Alas, his lot ! his lot of clothes are bad ;
Tattered and torn about his person view,
   And then thou'lt think of Homer and grow sad,
Or I mistake the sympathy that's due
   " The child of song" o'er sinful world's gone mad,
And then please draw from out thy purse a sum
To purchase Twist Tobacco, Tea, or Rum.*

---

* These verses were written, and printed on a sheet, with a view of relieving their subject during a period of great privation.

Gibbon were found in the same apartment. The lordly owner of Minsteracres, finding John the more balanced of the two, invited him to go and see him. Lough did so, and his patron showed him the works of Michael Angelo and Canova ; the former of which, according to his own statement, took great hold of his mind. This kind attention on the part of Mr. Silvertop, with other help more substantial, afterwards bestowed, had undoubtedly a most powerful influence for good on John Lough's successful career. Poor Tom often told me how jealous he was when the Squire entered the cottage lest John should claim some of his drawings, and remained in the apartment during the interview, occasionally calling the visitor's attention to some of his drawings, which, however, were not destined to make their author aught beyond a local name, nor anything in the shape of a living more than a few scant coppers to purchase the indespensable tobacco and tea, the latter of which was more to him than nectar to the gods, and sometimes a glass of something stronger. Alas, for comparison ! Here are two brothers, who started life with apparently equal chances, both with strong vigorous constitutions, and of similar education ; one died in London, after having made his memory immortal as a sculptor of undeniable genius, in wealth and affluence : the other, after roaming through the counties of Northumberland and Durham as an itinerant musician, poet, and artist, for more than fifty years, begging from, praising and cursing mankind, sleeping at night, in summer, in hayfields, sheds, caverns, or in deep dells listening to the voices of Nature, in winter by pit fires, in gas works, on the floors of inns, and the commonest lodging houses, but never in bed like an ordinary human being, died at Lanchester, and was buried in a pauper's grave, partly at the expense of the parish which gave him birth, and might have been rendered momorable by the genius which few will deny that he possessed, had it been used aright. The early part of Tom's career was spent near the head of the Derwent, as a blacksmith, sharpening " jumpers," or drills, for the leadminers, and afterwards in his father's blacksmith shop at Greenhead, in shoeing cattle with a sort of " cleat," which was then in use to prevent those animal becoming footsore in their journey from the north to southern markets ; but the rhythmic ring of the anvil did not suffice for the softer sounds of ever lovely Nature, nor the glare of the forge for the soothing lights of the shadowy woodlands, or the golden glow of the setting sun. So he left

But ere thou leav'st the presence of the Bard
  (For thou, I would, should'st know him thoroughly),
Just ask him, in a spirit of regard,
  To draw his papers, and reveal to thee
His touch artistic, as a meet reward '
  For timely aid and generosity ;
And if in wond'rous joy thou'rt not repaid,
  To grave *Miss Fortune* may I be betrayed.

by degrees this honourable means of making a living, and took to a life of roaming and privation, which ended as above described. A friend, who knew the Lough family well, told me that Tom commenced his wandering life as early as the year 1826 or 1827. When the engines for the Messrs. Annandale's paper mills were being laid down, the engineers engaged in the work used to frequent the Bridge End Inn, Shotley Bridge, in the evenings, where Lough often turned up to entertain them with the Jew's harp, and fiddle, and by reciting his own and the poems of other authors, and by airing his drawing talents. His *forte* was, doubtless, the latter, and had he persevered, we might have had a different story to tell. His favourite subjects in drawing were the " Ninevite Bull," "The Flying Ass," "Group of Bacchanalians," Byron's "Mazeppa," and a group containing two human figures and several savage-looking horses ; the latter of which I have in my possession, and feel sure that were it engraved it would preserve the memory of its authors from oblivion, for it is not only vigorously drawn, but is a wonderful conception, and, with other productions of his, shows how his mind, stored with the literature of Greece and Rome, teemed with imagery. His favourite authors were Homer, Virgil, Shakespeare, Gibbon, Byron, and Burns ; the first of whom he had read earliest and most earnestly, and in consequence his mind received the strongest of its colours from the great Greek. The parts of Gibbon referring to religion and politics he could recite almost word for word ; while the portions of Byron's " Childe Harold " which revel in the arts of Greece and Rome, and the great and glorious names of those empires, were to him a never-ending source of pleasure, wonder, and admiration. His performances on the violin were of the most comical character, and produced effects, according to his own accounts, that have never been equalled since Orpheus played his spouse from that region so much dreaded by many mortals. Placing the fiddle between his knees when in a sitting posture, he used the bow vigorously, and thence flowed strains which, as fame informs us, caused, in a certain inn, in Weardale, I think, panes to fly out of the windows, the pot lid to fly up the chimney, and a child to leap from the cradle of its slumbers, and dance in a most unaccountable manner. It was here, too, I believe, that he drew a fox with a piece of charcoal on the hearthstone, which the terrier dogs with the company attempted to seize, mistaking it for a living reality. Poor Lough used to tell me those absurd stories with a solemnity that could not be exceeded by the gravest Musselman. Lough's chief poems are " Chatt's Hare," " Galloway Jack," and " Ramshaw Flood," all of which show a fair amount of poetical talent, but lack rhythm. Among

Behold from Nineveh's wide fields of art
   Reflections of the mighty genius there ;
Enough to make a stone or Stoic start,
   To trace the life-like forms so chaste and rare ;
Thou'lt almost deem the actions of the heart
   Thou can'st discern in bosom bold or fair ;
Or see the wing'd ass in a milky sky,
Rather *unlike* a giant eagle fly.

his peculiarities was an utter hatred to the colour red, an aversion to looking-glasses, and a dislike to any room where there was a flood of light and strong reflection. He also disliked to see a hole in the wall, and would, if allowed, stuff it with paper, turn the looking-glass around, and cover up any shining ornament which offended his eye. These peculiarities of character, no doubt, sprang out of his very high temperament, his long acquaintance with the soft and mellow lights of the woodland, his natural home, which knew no fiercer reflection than the waters of the river, streamlet, or lake, placid or shimmering beneath a summer's sun. Lough once told me a story, which I had also heard from another source, of the great offence he gave to a blacksmith, near Castleside, by drawing his portrait whilst shoeing a wicked donkey, one of whose ears was placed in a vice to keep him quiet during the operation. It was exceedingly amusing to hear poor Lough recite "Ramshaw Flood" and "Galloway Jack," the latter of which he thought a better poem than "Tam-o'-Shanter," considering the materials out of which it was composed. He would start slowly, and with great attention to pronunciation and articulation, but would forget both as he became impelled by the fire of the pieces. On and on he would go, with his large wild eyes fixed on some inanimate object, astonishing his hearers with matchless volubility, till he closed with a jumble of sounds, out of which it was hard to extract a single word. The same wild eyes were then turned inquiringly upon the audience, and if anyone ventured to pass on the Bard condemnatory judgment, he at once became the object of a volley of epithets that Daniel O'Connell might well have been proud of, for poor Tom revealed a most powerful vocabulary of abusive language when in anger. In his poems there are many evidences of want of command of language, but when his indignation was roused it flowed from him like raindrops from a thundercloud. Lough, as I have shown, had wonderful talents, in fact he was a genius in his way, but he was not a balanced man. Had he fallen into some business more congenial to his nature, and into mind influences of a higher type, there can be no doubt that he would have made his " footprints on the sands of Time." But as conjecture in this case is vain as hope without action, we will leave poor Tom to his slumbers, and take warning from the results of his failings ; nor wholly despise the memory of him who possessed much in common with the greatest and noblest of minds—admiration of the highest artistic achievements of man, and a love of the peerless beauties of Nature so intense that no human language, however powerful, could express it.

See the " Mazeppa" bound, without remorse
 (Like a foul weed given to the tempest's breath),
Unto the bosom of the furious horse,
 Which bears him onward like a fiend of wrath.
The famished wolves assail his flying course ;
 Behold the languid form : Thou'lt deem that Death
Is stealing o'er his features. From thine eye
A tear shall steal,—thy breast shall heave a sigh.

Look, ere thou leav'st the subject, to the face
 Of the wild bounding brute, and not in vain
Thy cunning eye shall various passions trace :
 Fear, Desperation, Vengeance bound in pain
Which cannot be controlled. Then mark the grace
 Breathed in the glorious symmetry, and then
Marvel that human brains, like Lough's, should be
The gov'nor of so strange a destiny.

Now rest thine eye a moment, and prepare
 Thy soul for a sublimer vision, sent
Like Raphael's St. Cecilia, bright and fair
 To build her medium's earthly monument :
Lo ! Hercules, the god of strength so rare,
 Amid a group of savage horses pent,
Whose power to his were as the crawling worm
To the dread vi'lence of the Simoon Storm.

Like a Colossus see the mighty stand ;
 The King's wild horses are his playthings now,
Helplessly writhing, one in either hand.
 Mark the fierce brute in furious flight below,
And other figures Genius can command,
 Leaning around, whose bosoms seem to glow
With admiration of the immortal god
Who rules the things about him with a nod.

Next the huge bull, "lord of the lowing herd,"
  Savage in mood, yet beautiful as vast ;
Here Skill designed the figure it preferred :
  Then look, and look again ere it hath passed
Into Oblivion, like a deed or word
  Unwritten. Earth's the loser : shame to cast
Such works as this away, which should be rolled
With Art's best deeds, for lack a little gold.

See the big muscle, the elastic limb,
  The full eye and the harmony of form,
The Samson strength pent up so tight and trim ;
  Thou'lt almost deem his form, like thine, is warm,
And shrink as though thou felt too near to him ;
  Then forward draw again, as by a charm,
And every moment see fresh beauties shine,
And wish the artist's glowing gift were thine.

In aspect varied see the frenzied troop
  Of " Bacchanalians " free from gnawing Care ;
Some stand erect, some lean, and others stoop,
  Or fling their limbs, and gesture mighty queer :
In short, they are a most ingenious group.
  The Artist's eye but sees them to revere
The grasping skill which could at once design
So wild a picture, as grotesque as fine.

But ere thou takest a long and last farewell,
  Perchance, of him who charms thine ear and eye,
Draw from his wondrous breast another spell—
  A most enchanting spell—'tis Poesy.
In floods of pathos, and in fun he'll tell
  How " Ramshaw " felt the vengeance of the sky,—
Of Snowball's rants, and " Chat's " eternal hare,—
His own privations—mark how poets fare :—

Alas! the poet has no other choice
　　Than charm the world and suffer for his pains;
The heavenly lark trills his melodious voice,
　　And cruel sportsmen scatter wide his brains;
The thrush bids echoes wake and hearts rejoice,
　　The pleasure but a moment there remains;
Next view this same heart cherishing a will,
Alas! the thing the bosom loved to kill.

Thus the poor poet roams the world, where nought
　　Around he loves save Nature's comely brow;
Apart in feeling, and apart in thought
　　From the cold-hearted and unfeeling crew,
Who are with savage passions ever fraught,
　　And wait their coming meed of vengeance due;
Yet he who suffers for fair Virtue's cause,
Shall live for ever in her glorious laws.

So, Lough, though thou shalt pass away from earth,
　　As Burns and Bloomfield did, thou shalt not die.
Genius with Death contracts a second birth—
　　The birthright of an Immortality:
Man asks himself what Fame like this is worth,
　　When dust returns to dust, from feeling free,
But seldom finds a fit and proper answer,
For darkling lies the Future never man saw.

Cursed be the hand that wields on Genius' head
　　The rod of Persecution, and deprives
The gifted sufferer of a crust of bread,
　　Ta'en from the abundance upon which he thrives,—
Who wrongs the wretch while living, but when dead,
　　And Talent leaves its mark, and Memory gives
A rapture to the name, piles o'er his dust
The monument to him—he could not spare a crust.

Enough ! my humble lay is all but ended
   Of him whose life would pile a curious story
Of Love, Hate, Hope, Despair, and Madness blended,
   As storms and tempests with the sunbeam's glory ;
Who drank from Nature as through woods he wended,
   The softer hues, but hates thy colour, Tory ;
And, reader, should'st thou meet him, if a Red,
He'd wish thy colour changed, or thou wert dead !

Song.

H ! if in thy bosom, a moment be stirred
    A thought, the sweet offspring of pity for me,
How weak the expression of glance, smile, or word,
    To breathe the delight of my spirit would be !

I look not to Mammon for happier days
    Than those that were spent in the magic of youth ;
I seek not for blessings, in high-sounding praise,
    From those who would dare nought for Honour and Truth.

For riches may fly when the sun of Success
    Seems beaming in radiance and glory the while ;
And praises are fragile as bosoms they bless,—
    The rainbow best emblems the light of a smile.

I look to the spirit, though trembling like thine,
    Lest Sin's sable wing waft a shade o'er thy soul,
Which looks to the Truth as its object divine,
    Like the needle that quivers, yet points to the pole.

Oh! the Robin Sings Sweet.

OH! the Robin sings sweet on the green ash tree,
  Where the old Well used to flow,
But nothing he knows of the former glee
  Of the days so long ago:
Too youthful is he to sing or tell
Of the scenes around that sparkling Well.

On the morning bright, or gloaming gray,
  How many have gathered here,
To laugh the merry hours away,
  Or to meet the one most dear?
And the hills around with echoes rung,
As impassioned songs of love were sung.

Old Well! in thy waters pure and bright,
  How many a maiden fair
Has viewed, in thy mirror's glancing light,
  Her form and flowing hair,
Ere her vessel dipped, and the ripples flowed
O'er the dancing eyes and the face which flowed?

And older ones have hither come
  With aspect grave, I ween,
Which showed that Care had found a home
  Where serener looks had been ;
For the form had gone which cheered the breast,
And left it Sorrow and Grief's unrest.

The scene, how changed ! since those vanished days—
  The waters gone, the maids have fled,
And the Summer comes with scorching rays :
  'Tis but to shine on thy parching bed,
Where once a mirror of beauty shone,
And the spot is sad, and drear, and lone !

The Village Hiring.

A North of England Picture.

TO Sing it as it should be sung, The Hiring,
 Would cost the poet very many labours,
For 'tis a subject odd to tune one's lyre on :
  The wild grimaces, curious gestures, capers,
Which Folly stands with open mouth admiring,—
 Now shaking hands politely with neighbours,
The country lass we find in garments gay,
Industry has provided for this day.

Her rosy cheek proclaims Health's blushing reign,
 Her sunny aspect breathes tranquillity,—
A simple modesty which cannot feign—
 To Nature true ; the azure of her eye
Of heaven's hue ; her lips like sunbeams twain,
 Bright as the gayest tulip's, crimson lie
Before a row of pearls as dazzling white
As e'er was snow-wreath 'neath the strongest light.

He whom her smile has blest is by her side,
 Forgetting masters, horses, wages, ploughs,
The emerald fields he's pressed in wandering wide,
 The grazing oxen, and the harmless ewes ;
His theme is—Mary—when she'll be his bride !
 To hush the fears which in his breast carouse,
Concerning the grave proverb—" Many a slip
(You know its truth) occurs 'twixt cup and lip."

In his misgivings I have had experience,
 But this is not the place for a recital.
Perhaps 'twill be your lot to hear me hence,
 Though such like stories, maybe, wont delight all,
Nor might they be, indeed, the true criterions
 Of a superior hope ; but now, despite all,
" Like Bunyan's plodding Pilgrim, I'll progress,"
With fear my varied text will please you less.

Then comes the jolly farmer, whose complexion,
 Fanned by the free airs, wears a healthy glow ;
The maids are placed before him for inspection,
 "Like four-and-twenty fiddlers in a row !"
I don't admire the custom on reflection,—
 For free-born English girls 'tis rather low ;
But it has grown to England with the Tories,
Though brings not with its age as many glories.

He (the farmer) eyes with care each blooming lass,
 Or lad, just as his need directs, of course ;
Some questions put, you know, about the " brass,"
 They ask to plough or sow, to milk or nurse,
Few cav'lings as to sums or service pass,
 Closes the bargain, lest he might do worse,
And seals it with a glass of port or sherry,
O'er which they grow, no doubt, a little merry.

If e'er you gazed upon this varied throng,
　　You've seen some things, I'm sure, to wake your laughter : .
The ballad-monger pouring forth his song,
　　The screech-owl's voice had been a great deal softer;
The fiddle's groans and squeals blending among
　　A thousand other sounds which come unsought for,
To bless or curse our little cozy village,
And break the silence of this very still age.

A little anxious are the lads and maids
　　Until they've got their vital business over;
This done at length, all free they make their raids
　　On apples, gingerbread, and nuts; moreover
Beer, rum, and whisky, or aught that aid
　　Pleasure, including wild beasts under cover,
Monkeys, elephants, performing bears,
Which play the vengeance with their numerous cares !

The Showman, in full-feathered eloquence,
　　(Success inspires him) he exerts his powers;
" To Natural History he makes no pretence,"
　　Yet on this subject dwells for many hours :
" This tiger is—you'll see it at a glance,
　　The most remarkablest in this land of ours,
To which from the Vest Hingen Hiles 'e came,
The place called Bengal,—you will know the name.

" This 'ere's a coon, a native of America ;
　　The negroes 'unt them by the pale moon light
With jovial singing, pitched upon a merry key,
　　When triumph smiles and wakes their wild delight.
That there barboon has climed the trees in Africa,
　　And this 'ere cove's a panther which cries by night;
While yonder curious customer, the hape,
Was bred, brought up, and captured near the Cape.

"That soft 'aired gentleman, why, 'e's a possum,
　Sometimes pretends 'e's dead as any nail,
And truth I tell, Sir, you might take and toss 'im
　Over a 'ouse top by his bushy tail ;
If 'e 'ad senses you would think 'e'd loss 'em,
　But soon 'e turns up, 'arty, strong. and 'ail ;
He, the brave hypocrite, as you could show,
Would rather *die* than run from any foe."

"A strange beast is the 'possum, still more strange
　Was one I had not very long ago ;
There's not a lady 'ere more prone to change
　Her dress than 'e 'is colour, now aglow
With red, now blue, now green would range,
　Like waves athwart 'is skin ;—'tis even so :
'Es called the camelion, and he lives on hair—
A cheap food, stranger, hisn't it, that 'ere ?"

"He lives on hair," quoths Betsy, "why that's grand ;
　What kind of hair, Sir, does the animal eat ?"
"My dear, you 'ardly seem to hunderstand :
　'Tis hatmospheric hair—it hisn't meat !
Though you and hi live on it as we stand,
　Without it, Miss, we couldn't keep our feet.
I wonder what would take 'em from us ever?
I never eat no hatmospheric hair, no never !

"That helephantine beauty as you see,
　'Im with the small heyes in their sockets sunk,
'E is hendowed with great sagacity,
　Though looks as sage and serious as a monk."
"I say, Mr. Showman, is that he
　I saw the other day packing his trunk ?"
"O yes, Sir ! this is in my list of marvels ;
'E halways packs 'is hown trunk when 'e travels !"

" That Polar bear, so beautiful and white,
　　Was captured by McClintock's hexpedition
To the North Pole, (where frosts hare said to bite),
　　In search of Franklin, and for hexhibition
Sold 'im to me for your hexpress delight;
　　To make you 'appy is my sole hambition,—
Behold 'is Majesty before we sever,—
Aint he a beauty and a joy for ever?

" And now, my friends, the hexibition's hover;
　　I 'opes you're satisfied with what you've seen.
Pray tell the people, who outside may 'over,
　　Of these, my curiosities, I mean;
My wild beasts, 'armless as the turtle-dove, or
　　Paragon of hinnocence serene.
Good night! Wishing you hall well married, and
Fortune, 'ealth, 'appiness at your command!"

Now linked in couples, plodding home they go,
　　Discussing all the pleasures of the day,—
The dance, the dress, the marvels of the show,
　　Sighing " another Hiring's passed away,"
And wondering if they'll like their place or no,
　　Reaching their home with dress in sad array.
And since we've traced them to their parting place,
We'll turn our head to " screen the dear embrace."

I Think of Thee.

On the Memory of a Dead Friend.

WHEN lonely, sad, and Mem'ry flings
    Her darkling tempests o'er my mind,
As some huge bird whose mighty wings
    In motion leave a storm behind ;
When strolling 'neath the glorious moon
    Whose soft light floods the earth and sea,
And silence under midnight's noon
    With beauty dwells, I think of thee.

When on some beauteous face I look,
    Where Modesty and Virtue shine,
And read, as in a lettered book,
    Eternal.Wisdom's gift divine,
And muse on orbs where soul-beams stray,
    Or lights of other worlds I see,
I turn forgetful of their ray
    And liquid glance, and think of thee.

When contemplating Truth and Worth,
    The Courage which inspires the brave,
In what the noblest joys have birth,
    Through pointing o'er the gloomy grave,
The source which gives the soul its power,
    The glowing heart its charity,
When gazing on thy favourite flower
    I cannot choose but think of thee.

When blighted hopes become my theme,
   And Sorrow tells my fevered brain
How Life and Joy are all a dream,
   And Pleasure's smile is frail and vain ;
When Love, which lives through Death came down,
   Speaks to my breast no longer free,
Where spirit-stirring voices tune
   And sweetly blend, I think of thee.

Where God His gathered forms has laid
   In grassy tombs with flowers adorned,
And Sorrow seeks the solemn shade,
   And oft in sable garb has mourned ;
When blighted in its fairest bloom
   By Death the lily pale I see,
An offering for an early tomb
   Ere summer fade, I think of thee.

I think of thee when Fancy soars
   To that high central home of love ;
If Virtue seek those hallowed shores,
   In sceptred glory there thou'lt rove ;
How sweet the hope—the dream how dear,
   When Time hath set my spirit free,
To leave remorse and anguish here
   And mix eternal joy with thee.

Woman's Beauty.

IS not the smile on Beauty's face,
   Nor tints that brighten there,
Nor glancing eyes of darting rays,
   Nor lavish sunny hair;

'Tis not the symmetry of form,
   Enchanting to the eye,
The swan-like neck, the rounded arm,
   The breast where gods might sigh

To dwell and pass a languid hour;
   Nor is it costly dress
That constitute the highest power
   Of woman's loveliness.

It is the sweet, soft, sounds which flow
   In converse, of chaste thought,
The breast that shares another's woe,
   The humbleness of heart;

The hand that's lifted but to bless,
   The tongue whose accents soothe,
Lips that but know Affection's kiss,
   And Purity and Truth;

The eye that scans not faults to throw
   Into a vulgar ear,
But true to Pity's touch will pour
   Full many a briny tear;

The open brow that speaks of calm,
   The winning, frank address,
That constitute the highest form
   Of woman's loveliness.

forget-me-Not.*

THOU dream of life, thou hope in death,
    When dread Oblivion wraps the clay,
Which erst had nursed the vital breath,
    And quaffed and blessed the living ray ;
For thee, the poet's soul sublime,
    Pours rapture through his skilful plot,
Extolling virtue, gilding crime,
    Thou radiant star ! Forget-me-not !

The father stretched on languor's couch,
    Who knows that by to-morrow's sun
He shall be chilled by Death's cold touch,
    Time past, Eternity begun ;
The mother in her last farewell
    Of loved ones who had blessed her lot,
Feel in their bosom's parting swell,
    Thy language, fair forget-me-not !

* This small herbaceous plant, the Marsh Scorpion-grass (*Myosotis palustris*) is well-known to lovers of flowers as the emblem of affection and fidelity. The author deals more with what the word, or compound of words, forget-me-not, suggests, than this delicate and charming little flower itself, as will easily be discovered by the intelligent reader.

The sailor dares the booming main,
   The tempest's shriek, the raging waves;
The warrior braves the gory plain
   Where thousands find untimely graves;
Explorers pierce to realms unknown,
   And smile in Danger's face, I wot;
Ambition seeks a golden throne,
   Through dreaming thee, forget-me-not!

When Honour bleeds 'neath Slander's tongue,
   By creeping things infesting earth,
The passions for a moment strung,
   To thoughts of vengeance do give birth;
But Calm comes down and Anger flies,
   And Worth, though it be in a cot,
Upon the glowing truth relies—
   " Mankind and Heaven, forget-me-not!"

When Love's enchantments thrill the soul,
   And lover's mingle heart in heart;
The noiseless moments as they roll
   Too quickly tell that they must part;
What adoration fills their eyes
   (Soft passion! shall it be forgot?)
Now Rapture speaking in their sighs
   Says to each breast, " forget-me-not!"

Religion soars the Heaven's height
   Through dens of crime, disease, and strife,
With yonder beamy torch of light,
   Lit at thy fire, Eternal life;
And as the bearer fainting dies,
   His Soul, which knows no earthly blot,
Says through the language-gifted eyes,
   " O gracious God! Forget-me-not!"

O! Sing me a Song.

"O SING me a song," said a hoary Knight,
    To a maiden soft and fair,
"That will fill my soul with a keen delight
    And rid my breast of care;
But let its rhyme be of the olden time,
    Of a merit rich and rare.

"Thou art, alas! the only child
    My God hath left to me;
Then sing me a song, let the air be wild,
    And the strain as full and free ·
As the zephyr's sweep o'er the sounding deep,
    Or the songs of Syrens be.

"My daughter, thou hast thy mother's voice,
    And her motions every one;
But she became her Father's choice,
    And dwells beyond the sun.
Now slow rolls Time on his march sublime,
    Since that angel form has gone."

O! music had in sorrow's hour,
    On the soul of the gray-haired chief,
A thrilling and immortal power,
    Nor always brought relief;
For it lilts or mourns as the bosom turns
    To the spirits of Joy or Grief.

Then an ancient harp the maiden took,
   Whose chords for years had slept
'Gainst an antique wall, on a carved oak hook,
   Where the spiders and moonbeams crept ;
That magician hand could sounds command
   And by turns it rejoiced and wept.

It poured through that old majestic hall
   A medley of soft sounds,
Like the weird voice of the waterfall,
   Which from rock to rock rebounds ;
And it wakened thought with feeling fraught,
   That stung like the adder's wound.

It told the tale of former years,
   And the glories of her sire,
His martial deeds in Honour's wars,
   The love of his first desire ;
And the echoes rang as the maiden sang
   With more than her wonted fire.

The strain had wept itself to rest,
   And the maiden's cheeks were wet
As she turned to gaze on her father's face,
   Who in deathly silence sat ;
For his face was pale as the mountain hail
   Which a winter moon has lit.

She took his hand, but, O God ! the chill
   That o'er her bosom sped ;
" Had my simple song the power to kill ?
   My sire ! my sire is dead !"
She lifted the lid that his eyeball hid,
   But, alas ! the light had fled.

Hopeless.

 MARK her stand by a glittering stream,
  (In the hush of a Summer eve),
 Which shimmers in Sol's refulgent beam,
  Ere he takes of our earth his leave,
And the crimson clouds of the western sky
Have caught the tinge of his burnished eye.

Through the swaying boughs the breezes sweep,
 And they kiss the radiant tide,
Which seems to rise from slumbers deep,
 (As from sleep a beauteous bride,
All glowing from dreams of the forms she's won),
To bid farewell to the dying sun.

And songs of love from the warbler's throat,
 (Are poured to the balmy gale),
Which from crag to crag in echoes float,
 And a thousand joys reveal ;
And the troutlet's leap from his watery bed
The circling ripples above him shed.

But 'tis not on the shimmering wave to gaze
　That her footsteps hither rove ;
No charms for her has Sol's fair rays,
　And the calm she may not love ;
Nor can the hues of the blushing west
　Bring to her heart its wonted rest.

Nor whispering zephyrs can soothe her soul,
　Nor laverock's trill, nor linnet's song,
Nor soft-voiced echoes as they roll
　From hill to hill on the breeze along,
Nor the circling waves where the troutlets roam,
Can drive her griefs from their cherished home.

With steadfast eye on the waters bright
　She looks, but through torrid tears,
Nor on, nor within them, no laughing light
　In her burning orbs appears ;
For her darkling thoughts are in awful force,
And her breast is a hell where writhes remorse.

Now crowd the passions of all her past,
　And torture her fevered brain,
Till like the seas, 'neath a rushing blast,
　Her bosom heaves with pain ;
Now a mother's love is blended here
With a knawing sin and a wild despair.

Now the cherished hours of " love's young dream "
　In the light of her vision shine,
And a moment dazzle as they beam,
　And with Hope's enchantments twine,
But pallid turn in reflection's eye
And beneath the Truth decline and die.

A fluttering noise behind me near,
   I turn for a moment now :
But hark ! what noise is that I hear ?
   What ruffles the water's brow ?
A bubbling groan sweeps o'er my heart,
And thrills of horror through me dart.

The waves again are calm ; beneath
   A youthful form is laid,
Which early sought the sleep of Death,
   By Sorrow's ills betrayed ;
The first dark step—the nursing wrong—
'Tis but a line of the *old, old* song.

Spring.

AILY thou comest o'er mountain and plain,
Lake, burn, and river, and wide booming main,
Scattering wild flowers like gems on the green,
Giving a rapture to every scene ;
Filling with melody every grove,
Breathing through Beauty—Hope, Pleasure, and Love :
From youth's cheek the radiant roses must sever,
But thou in thy glory returne$t for ever !

Thou breath'st, and the storm-king is hushed to repose,
The air rings with song, and the flowers disclose,
The earth dons its em'rald, the heavens their blue,
And man's aspirations are nobler now ;
His eyes softly fall on the beauties of earth,
And thoughts of their Author like joys spring to birth ;
These flash on his dark soul as night-lightnings quiver,
The gloom still remains : Spring ! thou brighten'st for ever !

Fair Spring ! thou recallest the morn of life
Ere the calm of my bosom had perished by strife,
Or the world in its hollowness dawned on my soul,
Which Innocence held in her silken control ;
And wak'st with thy presence remorse and its pang,
As with a dark tempest my bosom were wrung.
Oh ! thus youth must fall into Time's silent river,
But Spring ! thou'rt eternal—thou comest for ever !

Thou com'st like a maid in the bloom of her charms,
Flinging around her enchantments and balms,
Robed in soft emerald, glowing with rays
Till animate nature awakes to her praise ;
And the accents of pathos like spirits go forth,
Flooding the world with her beauty and worth ;
Her bloom shall decline, spite of Virtue's endeavour,
But Spring ! thou return'st, and art lovely for ever !

Afar in a region no mortal hath seen,
Save with faith-gifted eyes ever calm and serene,
Where the tempests of Hate and the follies of Pride,
War, Famine, and Vengeance may never abide ;
There the soul hath her Spring, and no Autumn shall know,
All pure in her triumph and glory shall glow ;
No blossom will fade, nought affections can sever,
But, wedded to Love, she shall flourish for ever !

To A.E.L.

 Cannot but linger wherever thou art,
Thou gem of my fancy, thou queen of my heart;
Whatever the passions my bosom entwine,
In the sunlight of Joy, or in Sorrow I'm thine!
Ere Fortune had hallowed my lot with thy smile,
A lone restless pilgrim I roved o'er our Isle;
Nor all the enchantments its glories could show,
Could breathe to my spirit what thou can'st bestow.

It is not that wit in its flashes bursts forth
From thy lips that I gather the pride of thy worth,—
It is not the tinge of that lip, or thy cheek,
Which to Love-ravished swains such a passion can speak,—
It is not thy locks, which are beauteous in hue,
Or the snow of thy neck, or thy fair beaming brow;
'Tis the glances of Love, and thy Virtues alone
So entrancing, that make me for ever thine own.

The mountains pour rapture sublime on the eye,
As majestic they tower through the azure on high;
The flowers of the valley have charms for my soul,
The streamlets breathe music and joy as they roll,
The forests in Grandeur's solemnity nod,
And speak to my spirit, thro' Nature, of God,
Whose mighty creations give pleasure and rest,
But God giving me thee linked me e'er with the blest.

"There Lacketh Something Still."

HOUGH Winter, with his gusty snow,
　　Hath gone from mount and lea,
And the living rays of Spring bestow
　　A robe on every tree,—
The flowers unfold
Their leaves of gold,
　　Adorning dale and hill,—
Though Light and Love
Invest the grove,
　　" There lacketh something still."

Though lav'rocks lave the landscape fair
　　With living lays of love,
And thrush and blackbird (heavenly pair!)
　　Pour rapture through the grove,—
Though soothing shade,
In every glade,
　　Whence rolls the rippling rill,
Absorbs the light,
And breathes delight,
　　" There lacketh something still."

H

Though azure is the radiant sky,
  And warm our mother earth,
Where many a gem of beauty's dye
  Awakes to wonted birth;—
Though greener grows
The fern which blows
  By yonder sombre Mill,
And everything
To beauty spring,
  " There lacketh something still."

Though maiden's love my bosom bless,
  And drive away my care,
The rapture of her glowing kiss
  Can steal me from despair,—
Though Fortune's smile
My soul beguile,
  My breast with pleasures thrill,—
Though Summer comes
With sweet perfumes,
  " There lacketh something still."

It is the want of Faith which brings
  Our sad satiety.
The breasts of peasants and of kings
  Have been a prey to thee ;
And whatsoe'er
The joys we share,
  Are pleasures Earth has given,
And fade away,
As flowers decay,—
  " There's nothing true but Heaven."

Spirit of Beauty.

O ! SPIRIT of Beauty,
   How oft have I seen
The glance of thine eye
   O'er the flower-spangled green, —
In the dew-drop which beams
   On the brow of the rose,—
In the clouds of the dawn,
   And the evening's close ;
All Nature's impregnate,
   Fair Spirit, with thee,
And dear is the glow
   Of thy presence to me !

When the mild-breathing Spring
   Throws her mantle of green,
And gives to the streamlet
   Its shimmering sheen,
And wakes the wild warbler
   His love-lays to pour,
In symphonies sweet,
   Through the shadowy bower,
'Tis then I behold thee
   In all that I see,
For dear is the glow
   Of thy presence to me !

Where Virtue and Purity dwell,
　Thou art there,—
In the maiden's blue eye
　And her soft sunny hair;
Where Charity mild
　Takes her seat in the heart,
And rules, like a monarch,
　With magical art,—
Inspiring the deed,
　From all Selfishness free;—
How dear is the glow
　Of thy presence to me!

Thou Star in the soul
　Of the Poet, how sweet
His communings with thee
　In the lonely retreat!
Who treasures, deep-shrined
　In his innermost part,
The language thou breath'st,
　Until married to Thought,
When it flows to thy praises,
　Like rain on the lea;
Then dear is the glow
　Of thy presence to me!

Thy home, when Perfection
　Has crowned thee as Queen,
Is the soul of the Just,
　Far in Heaven's serene;
Which Faith, with her prophet-like
　Eye, shows us here,
Where nothing can mar thee
　Of Sorrow or Fear,
And Sin may not enter,
　But all shall be Free;—
How dear then the glow
　Of thy presence will be!

Lines Addressed to Mr. A. Prior on his

Bridal Day.

MAY Glory await on thy young, gentle bride,
  In whose full flush of beauty thou tak'st to thy
      breast :
Such bliss Alexandra alone has supplied
To our own noble Prince of this Isle of the blest.

You are worthy each other. While England reclines
  On her lineage—the brightest the world ever gave !
Thy country, Old Denmark, untarnished still shines
  With the Saxon and Roman—the best of the brave !

Oh ! make her a home in yon far Royal town,
  All radiant with gladness, to equal her birth ;
Dispel not one ray of her joy with a frown,—
  Let THY English maid crown the pride of thy worth.

When Gaiety's glories are mingling around thee,
    And other bright eyes pour their magic on thine,
Remember the eyes whose effulgence spell-bound thee,
    Twining rays into fetters of virtues divine.

And oh! let us charge thee, when Time's busy finger
    Has chased from those lineaments charms that abound,
To cherish her still, as when turning to linger,
    And strengthen in Love for some charm-hallowed ground.

'Tis Merry.

'TIS merry, 'tis merry, when Winter flies,
And Spring's first gale through the woodland hies,
And the first fair flowers from their prison wake,
Their odours abroad o'er the land to shake;
And the gush of song from the warbler's throat,
Like spirits of love on the soft airs float,
And Aspiration seizes then
The softening hearts of wayward men!

'Tis joyous, 'tis joyous, when Summer comes,
With her foliage dark and her thousand blooms;
And the lovely meadows their balms retain,
And cereals wave on the fertile plain;
And the liquid tune, by the streamlet played,
Is floating in echoes from glade to glade;
And Luxuriance reigns o'er the season's pride,
With hallowing Beauty for his bride.

'Tis solemn, 'tis solemn, to wander by
The mountain stream, 'neath an Autumn sky,
When the emerald folds of Summer's dress
Have changed, but to hues of loveliness,
Whose glorious tints breathe to the soul
The thrilling truths of a mortal's goal;
And Reflection gives to the wand'rer's breast
The promise—the hope of eternal rest.

'Tis gloomy, 'tis gloomy, when Winter frowns
O'er mountain, plain, and hazel downs;
When the whistling winds through the woodlands fly,
And dark clouds obscure the stormy sky;
When faint and weary the beggars roam,
Without a hope, and without a home;
And the poor lone widow and orphan share
The sorrow that springs from a cupboard bare.

O, mortal of thought! is it all in vain
That the seasons change, and the throbbing brain
Records the fact that Decay must come,
To quench the light and destroy the bloom,
And sweep from Beauty's galaxy
The fairest maid with the radiant eye?
And the strong and the wise to his laws succumb,
To sleep in silence within the tomb?

Napoleon 333.

FORLORN Napoleon ! in thy breast
  What passions revel now !
At length does thy ambition rest,
As a wounded eagle in her nest,
  Pent on some crag's bleak brow,
From which she gazes o'er the plain
Her pinions ne'er may stretch again.

Torn from the land thy greatness gave
  Another fadeless wreath,
O ! would that thou had'st sought the grave
Where moulder now thy vanquished brave,—
  Their honour shared in death !
Then sympathy had wept the throne
Divested of Napoleon.

But shame's exchanged for pomp and state,
  A prison for a crown ;
The land thou thought'st to desolate
Has stood the tempest of thy hate,
  And dashed thine eagles down ;
And France, who bore her head so high,
Nurses revenge impotently.

Thy splendour's past: in solemn calm
    Thou'lt thrill to dream the hour
When vengeance, in each peerless arm,
Assailed thy foemen as the storm
    Resistless in its power:
Now Austria's pale host shrinking yields
On fair Italia's blood-bought fields.

Then turn to Russia's sanguine walls;
    Does Glory greet thine eye?
With Albion gaze where Victory calls,
But nought thou'lt see in ruined halls
    Foreshadowing Destiny,
More than may breathe Ambition's fate,—
Stern lesson which thou'st learnt too late.

Too late thou'st learnt that men are things
    In guilt and guile arrayed,
Who kiss the feet of meanest kings
Whilst power unto their footsteps clings.
    Twice damned who thou betrayed;
If busy conscience does not kill,
Proud France may have her vengeance still.

Shall England's gratitude repose,
    Nor wake to weep thy fall,
And view the triumph of thy foes
With nought of Pity's rending throes,—
    When truth and friendship call
Back to the soul those deeds of fame
On which our mingling blood has claim?

Let those who mock thy power o'erthrown
    Remember thou hast been
The Monarch on as proud a Throne
As e'er was to an Empire known,
    And ruled as well, I ween:
Then feel no feeble brain could stem
The tide to such a diadem.

There are who weep thy spouse and thee,
　And mourn your glory gone;
She's worth thine immortality
If thou wert crowned with victory,
　And still possessed thy throne.
Thy friends are false, but she has proved
'Twas not thy power, but *thee*, she loved.

Then lean thee on her faithful breast,
　And hush Ambition's voice;
Sweeter shall be thy pillowed rest
Than when the beams of splendour kissed
　The objects of thy choice,
And know thyself, whate'er betide,
The husband of a glorious bride!

Lines on Hearing a Skylark Sing in February.

IKE a joy which has burst from its bonds of control,
To ravish the heart and to gladden the soul,—
Like the first beam of hope through the gloom of
    despair,
Or a smile o'er the face on the exit of care,—
Like a sunbeam which peeps through the bars of a cell,
On the bosoms of those who in sorrow may dwell,—
Like the first tear of love o'er the maiden's bright eye,
On the fond heart of him for whose sake she would die,—
Like the voice of an angel which, earthward being driven,
Breathes to mortals the bliss and the magic of heaven,—
Like the first glance of spring, when the storm-king has fled,
Giving rapture through beauty to woodland and mead,—
Like a hope springing out from the woes of the past,
To tell the sad heart of a blessing at last,—
Like all that is joyous, like all that is bright,
Thy song, heav'nly lark, thrills our souls with delight!
A lesson thou teachest—a patience revealest,
And through the dark tempests of winter thou feelest
There is something of gladness and pleasure to come:
The blue sky above thee—beneath, the fair bloom
Of the pasture and meadow, the woodland and glade,
By the hand of our Maker in splendour arrayed.
So, mortal, though winters and trials may come,
O'er their bier sunny spring pours a light and perfume;
And when life's tears and sorrows are past, we are given
A promise of glory for ever in Heaven!

happiness.

"Man never is but always to be blest."—*Pope*.

VIRTUE'S twin sister, lovely spirit thou !
  By every mortal wooed, by few obtained,—
Fair as the lily laved with morning dew ;
  When Youth and all its charms are yet retained,
Thou art the aim and end of life ! And how
  The struggle lingers, and the eye is strained
To catch one glimpse, or rest the longing gaze
Upon thy hallowed form, to ponder all thy ways !

Yes ! thou like maiden coy, with eyes of blue,
  Since hoary Time began his march sublime,
So man has sought thee as he seeks thee now !
  The Poet builds to thee the lofty rhyme,
The Sage with calm reflection on his brow,
  Divines, Philosophers of every clime,
Have told the world thy dwelling place, yet none,
Or few, have ever clasped thy chaste and tempting zone.

Yea! man has sought thee in the Dance, the Play,
   The Chase, the Field, where Battle's thunders roar,
And deems thou art in Victory's loud hurra;
   But may not find thee there, though high he soar
On Triumph's wings, nor in the lofty lay
   The Poet twines around his name and shore;
Nor where inglorious Patriots bleed and die,
For thou art not where Pity wipes her tearful eye.

And others seek thee on the breezy mountain,
   Where zephyrs bathe the brow and calm the heart;
Or quaff the mystic music of the fountain,
   Whose lullabies a thousand joys impart;
Or roam the twilight dell, their pleasures countin'
   In thought too deep for words, and deem thou art
A moment to be found with Nature there,
But flee as worldly dreams their wonted power declare.

Homer, Shakespeare, Milton saw afar
   Thy form through Glory on Parnassus' height;
Napoleon saw thee on the Conqueror's car,
   Riding with Triumph 'midst the stormy fight;
Newton beheld thee in each radiant star,
   Through Immortality's transcendent light,
In Heavenly visions, but at distance still,
As Poets see thee far upon the Muses' hill!

The love-lorn maid, in Hymen's silken knot,
   Espied thee shining loveliest as thou wert;
But Time rolled on, and there she found thee not,
   Except in Dreams, and Hope forsook her heart,
And fled the precincts of her humble cot
   With him whom Death had snatched with cruel art;
Pale Melancholy seized her trembling breast,
And laid her down to sleep with him she loved the best.

O, Happiness! thou art not earthly born,
    But art the spirit and the l'ght of Heaven;
Though transcient rays from thy bright face adorn
    At times our dwellings, as a foretaste given
Of that eternal Paradise, where morn
    For ever ling'ring shines on those forgiven,
Who wash'd their robes in the bless'd stream which flowed
On Calvary's sacred Mount from the Incarnate God!

.

.

A Prayer.

O GOD, whose all-supporting skill
   The weary wanderer guides aright,
Who yields obedient to Thy will,
   And prays for Faith's clear-piercing sight,
Give me the patience, calm serene,
   To thwart the fiery Tempter's power,
When Hatred's shafts are flying keen,
   To stand unmoved the trying hour.

Teach me, my Father, to subdue
   The bursting passions as they roll,
Like wild and raging tempests, through
   My agonized and yielding soul.
Give me, O Heavenly One! to know
   That Thou my only Friend canst be,
And Satan my eternal Foe,
   Whatever form he wears in me.

The Jealousy, the Envious thought,
   Ambition's pitiable pride,
And Anger, Wisdom never sought,
   But fain for e'er would seek to hide
The burning passion to be Great,
   Forgetful of my fragile form,
The nursing of an inward Hate
   'Gainst those who've sought my earthly harm.

Teach me to soar from earthly things
   To purer air and fairer clime,
On Love and Hope's aspiring wings,
   And know alone Thy love sublime.
Give me a foretaste of that Home
   Which yet appears as mortal dreams,
That I from Thee no more may roam,
   But drink my fill at Heavenly streams.

And leave below the ruder realm,
   The meaner thought, the tainting sin,
Where furious storms no more o'erwhelm
   The calm my bosom holds within;
Where I may hear the distant thud
   Of warring Ocean's boom beneath,—
Behold the dusky cloudlets scud
   Before the tameless Tempest's breath.

As soars the eagle through the clouds
   When lightnings flash and thunders roar,
And whirlwinds tear the groaning woods,
   And crash the waves along the shore,
So would my purer spirit rise
   Through all o'er all to calms afar,
And view from yonder tranquil skies
   The wrathful elements at war!

Say, Mary.

SAY, Mary, why that gloom—
　　That soul of settled sadness?
Has gay Mirth fled her home,
　　Joined by her sister—Gladness?
And left thee in despair,
　　With none to love and bless thee,
And chase from features fair
　　The thoughts which so distress thee?

I know he has not been
　　So much of late about thee,
And oft I've marked thy mien
　　Was changed, and thy bright beauty
Was fading ray by ray,
　　Till thou wert worn with sorrow,
And cheerless seemed thy day,
　　Nor hope breathed better morrow.

The streams, whose spirits fling
　　Their soft mysterious voices
O'er groves where wild birds sing,
　　And every heart rejoices,
Another's gaze may woo,
　　Another's breast make cheery:
There's nought in Nature now
　　Of love and light for Mary.

The flowers have ceased their smiles,
  The towering hills their grandeur;
No more the lark beguiles
  Thy willing feet to wander;
The moon has lost her charms,
  The stars their peerless brightness,
The meads their soothing balms,
  Thy gentle heart its lightness.

Thine eyes, where love and light
  Had made their kindred dwelling,
In azure glory bright
  Of slighted love are telling;
And he who sought thy heart,
  And won it through his feigning
A love which was but art,
  Mocks thee with cold disdaining.

He reads thy soul's sad lore,
  But heeds not torn love's sighing,
Nor heals the wound he tore,
  And laughs to see thee dying;
Exulting in thy woes,
  Remorselessly revealing
A fiendish heart, which glows
  With nought of human feeling.

Then throw him from thy breast,
  As a leaf by the tempest driven,
For they say he makes a jest
  Of those who speak of heaven.
And, since he's false to thee,
  Thy virtue should refuse him,
And it would leave thee free
  To dash him from thy bosom.

Then when thy vital thread
  Is snapped by Death's cold finger,
Above thy mouldering head
  Soft Sympathy shall linger;
And Virtue's friends shall come
  Where honoured worth reposes,
And strew thy silent tomb
  With daisies meek and roses.

How different is his lot,
  Whom Constancy has slighted!
No maiden to the spot
  By Truth shall be invited;
For who would weep the breast,
  Though low and lonely lying,
That blighted woman's rest,
  And mocked when she was dying?

Stanzas to the Skylark.

ING to the earth, O heavenly bird!
   Sing to a thousand 'raptured hearts;
Such pathos never mortal heard,
   Thy song imparts.

Sing, nor in vain, thy trembling strain
   Flows wildly through the azure dome,
And fills with joy the flowery plain—
   Thy fragrant home.

Oft have I strained a boyish eye
   When loit'ring by the shimmering stream,
To see thee climb the inviting sky
   In morning's beam;

Or when night's herald, sober eve,
   With crystal dews stole o'er the plain,
Of burnished day thou took'st thy leave
   With seeming pain.

Still dost thou lighten o'er my breast,
   And streak the gloom that lingers there,
As lightning flashes o'er the west,
   By midnight drear.

And I behold thee wandering still,
　A speck beside a snowy cloud,
And feel my soul with rapture thrill,
　Strong, sweet, and loud.

In thee mankind a lore may learn,
　Unmingled with that sophistry
With which the human mind will burn
　To gild the lie.

Thou tellest how weak are earthly creeds,
　Where subtle minds display their powers :
There's more that man obdurate needs
　In lovely flowers.

They speak without the power of speech,
　And breathe through Beauty's sunny face
An eloquence the soul to reach,
　Without grimace.

So, sweetest bird, the lesson taught,
　Though lowly born, thou canst aspire
To realms which, like the earth, thou'st fraught
　With Love's soft fire.

Stanzas to the Daisy.

To thee, sweet unassuming flower,
'Tis given beyond the Poet's power
  To thrill the Briton's heart,—
To bid within his bosom rise
A thousand patriot ecstacies,
  With tenderest passions fraught !

To call his soul to some fair dell,
Where first thou on his fancy fell ;
  Or drew his willing eyes,
Whilst lingering by some brooklet's braes,
Where fell the lav'rock's melting lays,
  Like angels' symphonies.

Or to the place that saw his birth,
Where thou begemmed the emerald earth,
  And first his footsteps roved ;
And Nature, in her fancy dress,
Revealed to him her power to bless,
  And make herself beloved.

With rapture still thy charm's control
I'll sing as painted on my soul,
　　From Childhood's earliest hour ;—
When wandering by the twisting burn,
O ! there e'en yet my mind will turn,
　　And thrill with Memory's power.

So turned mine eyes from other shores,
Where towers the pine, the cat'ract roars,
　　And mighty lakes expand
Like burnished realms of dazzling sheen,
'Rose in my breast each native scene,
　　O much-lov'd native land !

I mused on hours whose happy reign
Knew nought of sorrow or of pain,
　　When, Daisy, thou wert given
A lesson (wide in influence, too)
To teach, when thy meek eye and brow
　　Were firmly fixed on Heaven.

But when the tempest howls on high,
And Vengeance shakes the sounding sky,
　　Thou cover'st up thy head ;
And whilst the ruthless torrents pour,
Thou meekly bear'st the dreary hour
　　Stretched on thy lowly bed.

But fixed as purpose not in vain,
Thou lift'st thy cinctured brow again,
　　When Sunshine lights the sky,
Brighter than thou appeard'st before,
Again thou look'st to yonder shore
　　With firm unwavering eye.

So, mortal, when the storms of life
Wage o'er thy head their wonted strife,
  Nor shelter thou art given,
Bear meekly with the trying hour;
And when the tempests lose their power,
  Through Sunshine look to Heaven!

Lines to the Violet.

I F Beauty's hues were sought alone,
 Such as the rainbow's tints disclose,
Or those in gayest tulips shone,
 Or blush in every virgin rose,
Or such as shine o'er suns just set,
In thee they're found not, Violet.

But seek the worth that Virtue knows,—
 The Modesty which lingers here,—
The fragrance of the dew-gemmed rose,—
 The charms of that blue eye, whose tear
Tells of Love's star, which ne'er shall set,—
 In thee they're found, sweet Violet.

Chatterton.

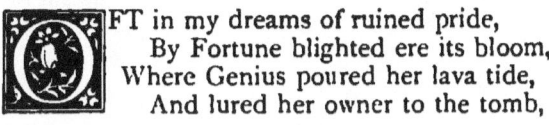 FT in my dreams of ruined pride,
   By Fortune blighted ere its bloom,
Where Genius poured her lava tide,
   And lured her owner to the tomb,

O ! Chatterton, of thee I've thought,
   And wept that such a glorious soul,
With hues of heavenly splendour fraught,
   Should find on earth so dark a goal.

Hard Fortune ! thou who sangst so sweet,
   Where golden Wealth revealed her store,
And ne'er a kindred spirit met
   To quaff thine all-immortal lore,

Should'st die by that same brain which gave
   Its " Resignation" to mankind,
And plunge in darkness to a grave,
   Yet leave such streams of light behind ;—

Light ! beauteous as the blushing rays
   Which hover o'er the gilded west,
When Sol withdraws his dazzling blaze,
   And sinks, as poets sing, to rest.

The soulless things ! they knew thee not
   (Else thou had'st lived to know thy fame)
Who broke thy heart ; they'll be forgot,
   Or live but in the voice of shame ;

Whilst thou on starry thought shalt soar
   The heavens' height—illumine earth ;
And men with pride shall claim the shore
   Which ne'er deserved, but gave thee birth.

·And sons of other climes shall read
   Thy glowing page as Time rolls on,
With pity for the Genius dead,
   And curse the foes of Chatterton !

In Memoriam.

Mrs. Isabella Turner, Died 17th February, 1881.

THOU art missed in the pew, there's a vacant chair,
For, alas! thou sit'st no longer there,
And tears dim many a burning eye,
Once radiant with the light of joy;
And sorrow dwells in many a heart,
Where love and hope had played a part
'Mong the varying passions which give to life
A zest to season the battle's strife.

There's a voice that is hushed,
   And a heart which is still,
Where pathos gushed
   Like a flowing rill;
There's a breast that heaves not,
   A pulse at rest,
A spirit which grieves not
   At woe's request;
And a hand reposed,
   By Death enthralled,
Which ne'er was closed
   When Pity called.
There's a veil that is drawn
   O'er a speaking eye,
Which awaits the dawn
   Of a brighter sky;
A prayer unsaid,
   Each day and night,
A Bible unread,
   And a Christian light
Fled from a sphere
   Of anxious care,
And toil and tear,
   To a clime more fair.

For thou had'st put thy trust in Him,
    The Lord of Hosts—the King of Heaven,
Before whose face all lights are dim ;
    Or as distant rays by a full orb given,
Which tremble in the dew-drop fair,
    Or shimmer on the streamlet's face,
And beam in Nature's beauties rare,
    And glow on the brow of the precipice :
So thou hast quaffed the streaming rays
    Of mercy from their Father flowing,
Which lit thee through earth's darkest ways,
    And kept a Christian bosom glowing—
(Celestial lights within thee burning,
    Whilst looking upwards to their Giver,
Like stars, the vaults of heaven adorning,
    Deep-mirrored in the crystal river)
Reflected—they reflect again,
    And were not given to thee in vain.

And though thy form's no longer near
    The region of thy wonted home,
Oh ! still thou art remembered dear
    By friends thou'st left below to roam :
And some would fain not linger here,
    But share the coldness of thy tomb,
Could they thy spirit's raptures know,
    Which from the God of raptures flow !

Thou art missed in the pew, there's a vacant chair,
For, alas ! thou sit'st no longer there,
And tears dim many a mourning eye
Once radiant with the light of joy.
And though earth's the poorer while ages roll,
Heaven is the richer by one pure soul ;
And our loss below is a gain above,
In the central home of Eternal Love !

Lines on the Death of a Very Dear Friend.

Geo. O. Rixon, Died December 17th, 1871.

AND shall thy bosom turn to clay,
   And not one breast its pangs record?
No! by the light of Virtue's ray,
   Thou shalt not pass from earth away
Unhonoured, undeplored!

(My lyre, though sad thy strain must be,
   Come throw thy murmurs o'er the gloom,—
Pour out thy burthen full and free:
With Pity touch his memory
   Who moulders in the tomb).

The mystic calm that wraps thee now
   Is sweeter than our tears and woes,—
We weep, and sorrow clouds our brow.
Alas! our pangs are vain, for thou
   Know'st nothing save repose!

Within our breasts thou shalt not die,
   For when we muse on truth and worth,
Thou shalt be first to meet the eye
That looks through cloudless friendship's sky—
   Thy greatest treasure, earth.

Thou shalt not die !   Immortal Grief
 Shall call thee from the hallowed dust ;
Nor give through time the wished relief,
E'en for a minute—(space so brief)—
 To heal the hearts which burst.

Enough ! since vain all sorrows prove,
 In radiant Hope we'll seek relief,—
Look to the central home of Love,
Where Purity is wont to rove,
 And nought is known of Grief.

The light we quaff at every gaze
 Shall banish anguish from our souls,—
Illumine with its heavenly rays
The depths of Sorrow's dwelling place,
 And seal the tear that rolls.

And when some vision of thy bliss,
 Like spirit-music sweeps our breast,
We'll turn to yon bright realm from this,
And drink thy joys, as moonbeams kiss
 The wavelet hushed to rest !

Reflections.

HE year is nearly worn out, John,
A wasted time to many an one,
A dreary void in chances given
For shunning Hell and gaining Heaven.
Another link to the sinner's chain,—
Some ten or a dozen may yet remain
To be forged and worn by the thoughtless slave,
As he rattles along to an early grave.
The path is beaten with foot-prints o'er,
For millions, alas ! have passed before
To the ocean that rolls without a shore.

The wise of all the ages past
Have a warning voice on the breezes cast,
In the solemn truths of immortal lore
Which point to the ocean without a shore :
But what is the lore of the wise to you,
My weary friend with the haggard brow ?
You have lived your time in passion and pain,
And the joys, O ! the joys, do they yet remain
Like the scattered flowers by the reapers spared,
In the parching stubble or emerald sward,
To be gathered and garnered in time to come,
When your better angel has ceased to roam,
And made your nobler heart her home.

J

You tell me Bereavement has left a smart
Which rankles and gnaws in your troubled heart,—
That Sorrow shall dwell for ever there
The boon companion of Despair,—
That you are weary, and fain would rest
By the ashes of her you lov'd the best,
And trust for a Future beyond the grave
To the turn of Chance or a favouring wave,—
That your life, a dreary and wasted hour,
Is flitting away 'mid the clouds that lower,—
That God, though in anger, your case shall weigh—
Your trials—temptations by night and day,
And brush your crimes from His page away.

O, desolate scene ! those wasted hours
Behind you cast like withered flowers !
And you are trav'ling a reeling swamp,
With " Will-o'-the-Wisp " for your only lamp,
With his flitful twinkle and feeble gleam,
Like the fire-fly's dance o'er an inky stream,—
Fit emblems of dying hopes, which fade
As frost-nip't flowers in an autumn glade,
Like a vision which told of a happier time,
When the heart, the heart was free from crime,
And Virtue rose in the soul sublime !

O ! dreary "wand'rer of mazes lost,"
Compassless mariner tempest tossed,
A turbulent ocean heaving round,
Each tow'ring wave with a foam-wreath crowned !
There is One can still this raging sea,
Who hush'd the billows of Galilee,
And is waiting with open arms to save
Your helpless form from the hungry wave ;
Then fly and lay your soul of grief
On His pitying breast and find relief :
Ask Him in faith for the glorious prize,
The life which lives when the body dies,
Beyond the mountains—beyond the skies !

Strayed from the Haunts.*

STRAYED from the haunts of the neighbouring
    poor,
A child was at play on the sea-washed shore,
    Joyous and merry, where few intrude,
Wrapped in her seeming solitude;
Charmed by the weird voice of the waves,
Listening the echoes within the caves;

---

* Mrs. Lucas, of Sunderland, in an excellent and chaste address on
Gospel Temperance, delivered in the Town Hall, Shotley Bridge, in
September, 1882, described, in her beautiful manner, an incident which
occurred one bright morning in the month of June, when, at an early
hour, she sauntered forth by the sea-shore, musing on the great question
which had taken such a hold upon her gentle and generous nature.
Far away along the shore, some distance from any human dwelling,
she came upon a little girl at play, moulding the sand into various fan-
tastic shapes, barefoot and hatless, her sunny hair fluttering in the balmy
summer breezes. To the right of her stretched the massive, towering
rocks, which had breasted the billows for ages: to the left, the mighty
ocean. The thought which awed her spirit on the bright morning of
that memorable day was—when these rocks are crumbled into dust, and
the ocean has ceased its throbbing for ever, the soul of this little child
will be living somewhere in God's great world. It is needless to say
that this touching and beautiful incident formed the text for the above
poem.

Watching the sea-birds' circling flight
O'er the dancing waves in the summer light;
Or some gallant ship on the ocean by,
Walking the waters in majesty—
Living, dear child, in the morn of life,
A rapturous hour before the strife
Break like a tempest, ere noon is high,
To veil the glory that lights her sky.

A lady, strolling the beach, beholds
The laughing child, as her scheme unfolds,
Shaping the sand to her fancy there,—
Building her castles in the air,—
And read, with eyes that Love had taught,
The lesson with which the scene was fraught;
And seeing the truth was realized,
Thus to her soul she soliloquised :—
" Child at play, in the early morn,
Fragile and fair as the hues of dawn ;
Pure as the balm of the summer rose,   .
Giving its life to each breeze that blows ;
Yet when the mountains to air have passed,
And the sea 's consumed in the fiery blast,—
When earth's foundations dissolve and fall,
And Chaos and Ruin are over all,—
When sun and moon and stars have fled
Their spheres of light, and are with the dead,—
O ! fragile child, before me at play,
Thy soul shall succumb not to dread decay,
But live beyond the bounds of Time,
'Mid brighter worlds, in a fairer clime,—
In light by God's own presence given,
And all the majesty of Heaven,—
Or where the unrepenting dwell,
In the constant pain of a torturing Hell.

" I go my way, and, as I go,
May deem thy soul has many a foe ;
And pray our God thy steps may guide
In Virtue's flowery paths of pride,
Religion's higher walks ascending,

Her grace and love with duty blending;
"That when the reaping time is come,
And Angels shout the harvest home,'
Thou may'st be found when the sheaves unfold
Their treasures, far richer than gems or gold.
And as the spangled dews adorn
The rose-leaves in refulgent morn,
So may thy deeds to Virtue sealed,
Their fragrance sweet and radiance yield,
Throwing their tender light afar,
Like glances from the morning star;
For all the wealth in the world's control
Is not worth the price of thy deathless soul."

The Passion's Power.

"He who the Passion's Power hath proved,
　Felt its alternate joy and pain,
He who hath well and wildly loved,
　Will love again."

ERHAPS the youth whose ardent flame,
　Dropp'd this warm verse as heaven the dew,
Linked to some soft enraptur'ng name,
　Experience knew.

Perchance the form he most adored,
　(Which for his own he fondly sighed),
Ere all its sweetness was explored,
　Had droop'd and died;

And left the memory of its joy
　Untouched, unsullied by despair,
Mingled of sorrow with the boy,
　To flourish there.

That memory, too, he fondly cherished,
　And fearful lest the passion fade,
He woo'd and won, ere it had perished,
　Some other maid.

But had he loved some faithless fair,
　Who laughed at all his bosom bore,
His heart had languished in despair,
　And loved no more.

In Memoriam.

John W. Muir, Died in Pietermaritzberg, South Africa,

October 30th, 1882.

TEARS flow, the heart is pained for thee,
 For Sorrow sits in silence there ;
Pale Pity bears her company,
 And shares the moment with Despair,
For thou in Faith and Love wert fair
As planets to the Shepherd's gaze :
Death tells that thou wert ever dear,
 And wakes the voice of honest praise.

How weak alike are Tears and Song,
 How vain the philosophic thought
To quench the grief—warm, gushing, strong,
 That thrills Bereavement's tender heart !
For thou wert not from us apart,
 Though distant far 'neath other skies,
But being of our being fraught,
 With all our loves and sympathies.

And Mem'ry shall her charms retain—
 On converse past her powers attest ;
As in some corner of the brain
 With dear delusive visions blessed,
Where oft the mental eye may rest,
 And live departed moments o'er,
So shall Reflection's eye invest
 Thy name with pleasures known before.

Sleep on within thy quiet tomb,
  Where, nurslings of another sky,
Fair flowers, unknown to me, may bloom
  To lure and charm th' enchanted eye,
And bright rills sing their lullaby, .
  And birds their lays to lis.'ning ears ;
But thine in silence steeped shall lie
  Unconscious of the rolling years.

Thou thought'dst to sleep in English earth,
  For thou wert born and nurtured here,
Where men who knew and prized thy worth
  Could pause, and drop the gen'rous tear ;
And genial May might scatter there
  The daisy with its cinctured brow,
Flower ever to thy bosom dear,
  Which may not bloom above thee now.

Nor may thy favourite skylark pour
  Celestial music o'er the sod,
Whence from the clay thy spirit pure
  Passed eagle-like to meet her God :
To see created joys abroad,
  And know the glories Heaven can give,
And tread where Christ Himself hath trod,
  There through Eternity to live.

Away, then, with our Tears and Woe,
  'Tis but a change that we call death ;
Nor bid the wells of Sorrow flow,
  Which live but where the clay has breath ;
Thou art not dead to eyes of Faith,
  But dwell'st upon a fairer shore ;—
" We'll meet," Hope's vital promise saith,
  To mingle there for evermore.

In Memoriam.

Mark Wall, died October 8th, 1871.

IKE the last ray of Hope that embellished thy
       pillow,
     And, flitting here, flattered the friends of thy
       heart,
Like the sunbeam that brightens the brow of the billow,
   Ere tempests their death-dealing vengeance impart,
Thou, my friend, hast departed : nor sunshine to-morrow
   Shall traverse the gloom which encircles the soul
Of those who may dream, in their silence and sorrow,
   Thy virtues, which point to a glorious goal.

Not in vain hast thou lived, nor in vain hast thou perished,
   For kindness and goodness exist not in vain :
'Tis these that will make thee eternally cherished,
   And speak to our bosoms again and again.
As the spirits of Dreamland preside o'er our slumbers,
   And call up the joys and the woes of the past,
So thy voice, though no more, shall awaken the numbers
   And echo its tones when I listened it last.

Yet Pity thy name shall environ with sadness,
   Which Time may reduce, but can never destroy ;
While Memory will call back the light of thy gladness,
   The warm gushing passion which ravished the boy.
Farewell ! though there's nothing so selfish as Sorrow,
   And sweet the repose of thy spirit may be,
We'll envy thee not, but reflectingly borrow
   The beam of thy bliss, and enjoy it with thee !

Lines on the Franco-German War.

I'M gloomy wi' the thought o't, Jean,
 I'm wae for a' the dead,
For mony a battle-field I've seen,
 Where hissed the awfu' lead ;
But never ken'd a war like this
 For nickin' life's frail thread.

I hae stood for my native land, Jean,
 Where poured the iron hail,
And hae heard on every hand, Jean,
 My comrades dying wail,
And hae wept the cost o' victory,
 Wi' cheeks sae cauld and pale.

Though o' British valour proud, Jean,
 And vain o' my Scottish birth,
For there never were men as good, Jean,
 To battle e'er went forth,
Yet I look on war as a curse frae God
 To punish this wicked earth.

(For our minister oft has said, Jean,
 That the curse and wrath o' God
Are administered through the aid, Jean,
 O' sinners who wield His rod ;
And mark, the medium o' his ire
 He never makes the good.)

Such passion is pride o' heart, Jean,—
  And promises nought but strife,—
It is aimed like the murderer's dart, Jean,
  At the fountain o' mony a life:
In its dried-up channels o' anguish die
  The succourless child and wife.

The widow and orphan's sorrow, Jean,
  Is so vast to my frenzied brain,
And grows wi' each dawning morrow, Jean,
  The gory piles o' slain,
Till they seem to mock at our sympathy
  As a worthless thing and vain.

It seems as though the earth and sky
  Were reeling a' wi' hate,
And Vengeance, wi' his crimson eye,
  Was monarch over fate,
And viewed the carnage mountains
  Wi' fiendish joy elate.

And darker gather the clouds, Jean,
  Ower what was sunny France;
Like the sough o' the winter woods, Jean,
  The conquering hosts advance;
And the world awaits the shock as though
  'Twere smittem wi' a trance.

Yet nane raise the arm o' defence, Jean,
  To stay the fatal hand
That hangs like a pestilence, Jean,
  Above the noble band,
Wha can calmly face the pangs o' death
  But shame can no withstand.

Has England her prestige lost, Jean ?
    Do her mighty minds of yore,
(O' which men are wont to boast, Jean)
    No longer rule her shore ?
Is her clarion voice for ever dead—
    Shall it speak to the world no more?

The nations are waiting her word, Jean,
    And would harken her counsel still,
For Rapine, that gory lord, Jean,
    O' slaughter has had his fill :
Then O ! would England speak aloud
    And the armies would cease to kill.

For I'm gloomy wi' the thought o't, Jean,
    I'm wae for a' the dead,
For mony a battle field I've seen,
    Where hissed the awfu' lead,
But never ken'd a war like this
    For nickin' life's frail thread.

Stanzas on the Death of a Child.

 SWEET be thy slumbers, and hallowed thy
      rest,
  Where the wings of thy spirit hath borne
      thee,—
Where lifeb-lighting tempests may ne'er touch thy
    breast,
  Nor soil the ·pure robes which adorn thee.

Thou art gone, like the pleiad that 'erst decked the
     sky,
  From the clasp of the arms which have bound thee,
But the faith and the hope that we'll see thee on high,
  Throw their soul-soothing influence around thee.

Like the rose which this morning embellished the
     thorn,
  The flower of thy cheek was in blossom,
Till Death's chilling frost had relentlessly torn
  And damped all the fires of thy bosom.

And now thou art laid in the deep silent grave,
  Where those love-bright and eloquent eyes,
Like stars shall arise to illumine thy cave,
  Or light up thy path to the skies.

There unfettered and free as a sunbeam thou'lt rove,
  Where no shadow of sorrow can stray,
'Neath the soft beaming glance of the Father of Love,
  And the splendour of limitless day.

Then weep not, bereaved one, Oh! weep not, 'tis vain
  All the heartrending throes of thy breast;
Thy child is exulting from sorrow and pain,
  " 'Twould be sinful to weep for the blest."

A Bridal Wish.*

HAPPY, happy, may you be,
　　Dear Lady o' our bonnie vale ;
And happy, happy, too, be he
　　Wha tauld you love's enchanting tale !

Though he has stown our fragrant flower,
　　Which grew by Derwent's sunny braes,
To shed perfume in Scottish bower,
　　And happiness breathe ower his days.

The widows miss your liberal hand,
　　The orphans want your kindly smile ;
But far in your romantic land,
　　You aye shall ithers cares beguile.

Yes, many bless your open hand,
　　And ower you're leaving shed the tear—
The tender tear—you'll aye command
　　Frae eyes that hold fair Virtue dear.

The vi'let, in its early birth,
　　Smiles sweet through its delightful blue ;
So shines the pride o' modest worth,
　　Which finds a cherished home in you.

* "The marriage of the Rev. W. Wood, of Campsie, Stirlingshire,
with Miss Annie Gilespie, eldest daughter of James Annandale, Esq.,
of Shotley Grove, was celebrated amid great rejoicings, at Shotley
Bridge, last week."—Newspaper paragraph, May, 1872.

Oft hae I passed you by the way,
　　An hundred times at least, I vow;
You little kent the thought I'd hae, ·
　　When aiblins I fogot to bow.

I thought (but something almost says
　　" You should na breathe what you desire")
That in the aspect o' your face
　　I trace the spirit o' your sire.

Your honoured sire ! (I speak it plain,
　　For truth has aye the strongest part)
Too noble to be proud or vain,
　　And rich in his great generous heart.

It is enough o' worldly praise
　　To say *you're his*, and emulate
His bounteous hand and kindly ways
　　To those who're born to poor estate.

So, Lady, may the winged hours
　　Waft blessings ower your worthy breast ;
And happiness with you and yours
　　Reign in your home—a welcome guest.

Then merry, merry, may you be,
　　Afar from this—our bonnie vale ;
And merry, merry, too, be' he
　　Wha tauld you love's enchanting tale.

To-Morrow.

THOUGH summer has fled, and rude winter
        is here,
    Away with the gloom of dejection,
    'Tis folly to murmur and shed the salt tear,
Though thy past has no charms for reflection.
If the thorns of thy path have outnumbered the rose,
    And joy has been quenched by thy sorrow,
Awaken thy hopes from their depth of repose,
    And bliss may enchant thee to-morrow.

Though lonely thy lot, since the soul of thy love
    Hath ceased to be troubled for ever,
Her spirit doth rove in the realms above
    No more from the blessèd to sever ;
And there is a joyance, felicity rare,
    With legends of happy before her,
She's awaiting thee now, so away with despair,
    Thou—immortal—mayst join her to-morrow.

If dark disappointment steal over thy breast,
    And Fortune rewards not thy labour,
While Honesty's crushed in thy bosom distressed,
    And wealth crown the hope of thy neighbour,
Frown not on the blessings another may have,
    But brush from thy brow every furrow :
Base envy belongs not to hearts that are brave,
    Be hopeful, and triumph to-morrow !

The brave and the good have a battle to fight,
    For sin howls his curses around us,
And though short is the triumph of Wrong over
        Right,
    The odds are inclined to confound us;
But who dies in a battle for Freedom, I wot,
    His memory ne'er wants an adorer,
His past and his present, they are not forgot,
    And victory shall crown him to-morrow!

'Tis not the possession of silver or gold
    That makes us the better or wiser;
No mortal's so wretched as him who grows old
    In worshipping Mammon—the miser:
He lives for himself, but he trembles to die,
    For death to his breast bears a horror;
He dare not ask God for a mansion on high,
    For he'd trusted Him not for to-morrow!

Contentment be thine, then, nor envy nor hate
    Allow to unsettle or grieve thee;
To bear, it is said, is to conquer our Fate—
    Philosophic and true this, believe me.
If poverty render too scanty thy board,
    And strength pale a little before her,
Know anguish oft gnaweth at Luxury's Lord,
    And thou shalt be painless to-morrow!

Though tyrants assail thee, fools laugh at thy lot,
    True worth hath a pride worth possessing,
And despot and fool shall alike be forgot,
    While thy name shall be breathed in a blessing.
I speak not in scorn of the wealthy and high,
    Some are noble in joy as in sorrow;
And if clouds of to-day dim the light of their sky,
    May it shine in full splendour to-morrow!

I know (as thou know'st) those of honour and worth,
 Whose talents and virtues adorn them,
And though Fortune and Nature have smiled on their
   birth,
 The poor on their exit shall mourn them.
To emulate such be the aim of thy soul,—
 A tithe of their wisdom to borrow,
Shall lead to the glory that shines in their goal,
 And it may be forthcoming to-morrow!

To spend the last portion where pity may call,
 To soothe in the moments of sadness,
To raise from the earth if thou canst those who fall,
 And tell them that virtue is gladness:
To succour the orphan—the widow to cheer,
 When bereavement a gloom has cast o'er,
Might be deemed by the selfish a folly, I fear,
 But Fortune may shun them to-morrow!

The children of Virtue have little to fear,
 Secure in the calm of their bosom:
The flowers of such soil to humanity dear,
 Shall give joy to the world in their blossom.
God save thee from Vice, whose enchantments for
   youth
 Lead thousands, I ween, to adore her;
So be pure, firm and noble, embracing the truth,
 And look forward with faith for to-morrow!

A Prologue.*

FRIENDS, patrons of our cause, when we shall
    tune
    Our gushing voices to recite or sing,
      Let's trust, like warblers of the grove in June,
Whose trembling pipes their soothing pathos fling,
Lend us your ears, we shall return them soon
    Uninjured, save their drums may jar and ring,
And if we please you and excite your laughter,
We shall have gained the object we are after.

There are who think to laugh is very wrong,
    And walk the earth with faces grave and blue,
Drawn out by mimic sadness, till as long
    As any washing-day you ever knew ;
Who treat a mirthful wight with language strong
    As Durham mustard, and as biting too,
And look upon our Dickens', Lovers', Sternes',
As wicked men, who should be hung by turns.

For why? Because they've urged the world, no doubt,
    Grow merry and rejoice 'neath loads of Care,
And made the wheels of life pursue their route,
    Which might have clogged with sorrow and despair.
Yet there was centred in their souls, not mute,
    The spirit of religion pure and fair ;
The wretched seldom asked their aid in vain,
For fun can melt beneath a tale of pain.

* The above prologue was delivered at Castleside, in 1870, at an
entertainment in aid of the fund for repairing the Day School there.

Deem not because the words of lightness fly
   From joy-o'erburthened lips to ravished ears,
That seriousness awakes no fear-born sigh,
   Or that such heart no sacred theme reveres.
'Tis said " the springs of rosy laughter lie "
   In " close connection with the well of tears."
Just now we'll take the laughter, and await
The well of tears, which never comes too late.

Music.*

I MIGHT have sung how Jubal, Lamech's son,
The tuneful art in earliest times begun,
Ere yet the awful deluge made the world
A watery sepulchre, to ruin hurled :
How in the anvil's rhythmic ring he found,
'Tis said, inspiring music's magic sound,
From whence the sweet-tongued lyre created came
To cheer his soul—immortalize his name.

Or how the leisure-loving shepherd heard
The whistling grasses by the tempest stirred ;
And eke he gathered from the wild bird's song,
The imitative thought, and, ere 'twas long,
Gave to the world his pipe, which, played wirh skill,
Tells of Arcadian groves and pleasure still.

Or how, when Pharoah's legions found a grave
Beneath the surging of the ocean wave,
Smitten of God, beneath His frown they sleep,
Fair Miriam's voice, swift-winged, flew o'er the deep,
Blended with timbrel tones, which ever tell
How Israel triumphed, and how Egypt fell.

Or how, when Salem in her glory rose,
Without a rival 'mong her powerful foes,
When all the hills and plains our Saviour trod
Were bathed in fragrance 'neath the smile of God,
The tuneful David's harp poured forth his soul,
And, like his psalms, which down the ages roll,
Sweeping and thrilling through the nerves of men,
Sought to subdue the heart, nor sought in vain :
In David Hebrew song its zenith found,
Which stands, like heaven's decrees, eternal and pro-
        found.

* These stanzas, in which the origin of music is traced, were recited
by the author on the occasion of a musical festival at Shotley Bridge.

I might have sung, but Time will stay for no man,
On music of the Egyptian, Greek, and Roman;
How Orpheus from that awful region, where
The wicked writhe in darkness and despair,
Brought back his spouse by music's matchless power,
The lute his instrument—and fame his dower.

But when I've sung, as verily I might,
If Time were flying not on pinions light,
Of Rolla's fire, and Paginini's art,
Which teamed such rapture o'er the trembling heart
Of Handel, Mendelssohn, and Mozart's right,
To invest the pealing organ with delight,
And send their names on Fame's proud wings afar,
To light the sphere of music like a star.

When all the instruments by man designed,
Are present with their varied strains, my mind,
Were it to choose, I'm pretty sure its choice
Would fall upon the liquid human voice:
So deep its pathos, and so sweet its tone,
A heaven-born instrument—it stands alone,
And here we have't in plenty to dispense
The sweetest sounds, and shall at once commence.

Sitting Alone.

SITTING alone where erst I sat,
　　By my native stream in boyhood's years,
Dreaming on changes since first we met,
　　Telling the tides of my toils and tears,
Since life was a Joy and Hope was young,
And my heart to other themes was strung.

Sitting and musing with feelings strange
　　On those dear companions of my youth,
O ! here is sorrow, for sorrow's in change,
　　They promised me constance to love and truth :
Now where are they who have with me roved
By the meadows fair and the paths we loved ?

Chasing the birdling, gathering flowers,
　　Wantonly wading the crystal stream,
Flinging its waters, whose misty showers
　　Framed rainbow tints in the sun's fair beam,—
Shouting where Echo returned the sound
With his mellow voice, to our joy profound.

Watching the lav'rock's winnowing flight
   Till he seemed but a speck in the calm blue sky,
While soft as the air of a summer night
   Fell the voices of raining melody
On the ravished heart, like a deep-fraught spell,
Where the tones of its gladness shall ever dwell.

How dear our youthful memories grow
   As the years with noiseless pace roll on !
They burst from their shrine away below,
   And glitter like streams in the morning sun,
Looking through human doubt and fear,
As the burning stars through the dark clouds peer.

O ! ever thus shall my early joys,
   Youth's friends, scenes, passions fill my breast,
Till Time, whose numbing touch destroys,
   And sets the pulse of life to rest,
And ushers the dawn of another sky
To canopy immortality !

Sitting and musing with feelings strange,
   Mingled with gladness in sorrow lost,
Because in the glance—my spirit's range—
   I miss the forms I had loved the most,
Which lie 'neath the turf by dasies spread,
Unmoved by the lark's song overhead.

Sitting alone by the spreading thorn,
   Crowned with blossom in June's first days,
Where the thrush through the early hours of morn
   Pours forth his 'rapturing songs of praise,
Which echoing die in the distance dim,
Like the fainting strains of a holy hymn.

My native stream, though far I've roved
   In lands beyond the ocean's wave,
Mid scenes and forms my bosom loved,
   Dear as the light—the fair, the brave,
Where the breezes ring with Freedom's voice
And men in Liberty rejoice,

I love thee still—shall ever love
   The tender memories of my youth,—
Thy hawthorn shades and willow grove,
   The friendships formed in changeless truth
Shall fade not, though by Fate's decree
I wander far from home and thee !

Neville's Cross.

Ballad on the Battle of Neville's Cross.*

IN conscious strength, with haughty tread,
    King David's army comes,
For Scotland's sons for honour's crown
    Have left their native homes,
And proudly toss their sable plumes :
    Their brilliant armour gleams,
And, like the light from summer's sun,
    A flood of radiance teems.

* A mile to the west of the City of Durham, are the remains of an
old cross, called Neville's Cross, erected by Ralph Lord Neville, to
commemorate a remarkable battle fought here on the 17th of October,
1346, in the reign of Edward III, between the English and Scotch
armies, called the Battle of Red Hills, or, as it has been subsequently
termed from the above erection, the Battle of Neville's Cross. In that
year, whilst Edward III was prosecuting his victorious career in France,
David the Second, King of Scotland, having collected a powerful army
of 30,000 men, invaded England by the western marches, showing tokens
of a bloody mind in the outset by putting the garrison of Liddell Tower
to the sword, and, with strange inhumanity, causing the noble knight,
Walter Selby, the governor of it, to be beheaded on the spot. After
burning the Abbey of Lanercost, the Scots pursued their usual route
through Cumberland and Tynedale. They sacked the Priory of Hexham, and afterwards entered the county of Durham without meeting
serious opposition. Measures were concerted for opposing the invaders,
and a body of troops, numbering 16,000 men, was assembled with the
greatest expedition. On the 16th, the day preceding the battle, David
lay at Beaurepaire, or Bearpark, while the English army was encamped
in Auckland Park. At nine o'clock the following morning, the armies
being in sight of each other, the Scottish trumpets sounded the advance.
The Scots were divided into three divisions : the first was led by the High

Far Liddell's Tower has felt their rage,
　　And yielded to its spell;
Here gallant Selby's soul of fire
Was quenched with all its burning ire,
　　And heaved its parting swell.
Where Lanercost's gray Abbey reared
　　Its sombre form on high,
The ashes yet with rapine warm
　　Of ruined grandeur lie. ·
See on the Cumbrian hills afar,
　　They urge their eager way;
Now Hexham's Priory they sack,
　　But spare the buildings gray.

Steward of Scotland and the Earl of March ; the Earl of Murray and
Lord Douglas commanded the second ; and the third, consisting of
choice troops, in which was incorporated the flower of the Scottish
nobility and gentry, sustained by the French auxiliaries, was commanded
by the King in person.   The English distributed their forces into four
bodies : Lord Henry Percy, victor of Hallidon Hill, supported by the
Earl of Angus, the Bishop of Durham, and several northern nobles, led
the first ; the second was led by the Archbishop of York, accompanied
by the Bishop of Carlisle, and the Lords Neville and Hastings ; the
Bishop of Lincoln, Lord Mowbray, and Sir Thomas Robeby led the
third division ; and at the head of the fourth was Edward Baliol,
supported by the Archbishop of Canterbury, the Lord Roos, and the
Sheriff of Northumberland.   Historians agree that the ground whereon
this battle was fought was ill-chosen, being hilly and intersected by field
enclosures, which considerably retarded the movements of large bodies
of men.   However, the Scots came on, and by dint of sword and battle-
axe they hurled the first English column back.   But Baliol, rushing in
with a body of horse, threw the Scotch battalion into confusion, and
gave the English time to rally and regain their ground.   The Earl of
Murray fell at this juncture, and Sir Wm. Douglas was taken prisoner ;
and the division seeing their leaders fall, fell into disorder, and took to
flight.   But the fate of the day was not decided, for the other two
divisions of the Scots stood their ground, and for three hours naught was
heard save the clash of arms, the breaking of spears, the muffled twinge
of the bow as the archers played their deadly cloth-yards,—those famous
six-feet bows, which won for England imperishable glory on many a
bloody field in Scotland and France,—the thunder of the charging
squadrons, the hoarse shouts of the combatants, mingled with the cries
of the wounded, and the groans of the dying.   David himself fought
with the courage which hope lends to despair.   He was, however,
disarmed, and led from the scene of carnage.   On the fall of the royal
banner, the Scots gave way, and made good their retreat, but not till
15,000 of their comrades slept their last sleep on the field.   The Cross
erected to commemorate the English victory remained standing until
1589, it which year it is said to have been defaced and broken down.

Still on they come o'er mount and glen,
    Relentless as the storm,
Till Derwent's sheltered banks are gained
    Of many a sylvan charm.
A night they linger on the spot
    Where once the Roman roved,
And dream, no doubt, the hallowed shades
    The Saxon virgin loved.
But restless as the fallow deer
    When hunters track his lair,
Behold them now by Beaurepaire,
Where roll thy waves pellucid Wear,
    And England's bravest dare.

In pomp and pageantry of war
    The King indulges now,
But conquest speaketh in his eye,
    And curls his warrior brow.
Now round him Desolation stalks,
    As led by fiendish powers,
And Durham in thy precincts now
    A dread destruction lowers :
The blazing cot, the bridge, the tree,
    Send up their flames on high,
And wanton like the lightning's wing
    In midnight's radiant sky.

Davies, however, in his " Rights and Monuments," fully describes it.
A drawing of the Cross was made and engraved for Hutchinson's
History of the County Palatine, printed in 1787, which agrees with
Davies' description, and may, we think, in the general features, be
accepted as a fair representation of the original erection. For the loan
of this beautiful little block we are indebted to the courtesy of Mr. Geo.
Walker, author and publisher of the Guide to Durham, whose father,
at the beginning of this century, lent it to Surtees to embellish his
magnificent History of Durham. It is believed that the block was cut
by Thomas Bewick,—at least, the elder Mr. Walker used to say so, and
he possessed a large number of the famous engraver's woodcuts. The
only portion of the Cross now remaining is the octagonal stone, or boss,
referred to by Davies as supporting the Cross. The pillar let into it is
no part of the original erection, having evidently been placed there in
modern times. At the latter part of 1883, Mr. Dodds, of Rokeby Villa,
solicited subscriptions for repairing the Cross, and the public responding
liberally, the mound on which it stands has been repaired, and the boss
has been placed on a stone base, a strong iron palisade, let into a neat
low wall, protecting the whole.

But where are Albion's hardy sons
　That erst no foe could tame,
Who conquered or conquering have left
　An honoured—deathless name?
Have Briton, Roman, Saxon, Dane,
　And Norman blent their fire,
To yield their blood-bought laurels now,
　And craven-like expire?
Where is that more than mortal pride
　In patriot souls which bled
On Hastings' sanguine field, or piled
　There mountains of the dead?

Fear not, my muse; in yonder Park*
　Some sturdy warriors lie;
Still burns the fire of chivalry
　In Percy's eagle eye,—
The hero soul which Victory bore
　Through Hallidon's fierce fight,
Where foemen fell, as summer rain
Descends upon a dusty plain,
　And sank in endless night:
The offspring of a noble race,
　Who strode by Rolla's side,†
By prowess on to victory led,
Or side by side with honour laid,
　And crowned with glory died!
In Neville's arm is deadly strength
　The flashing sword to wield,
And Copeland‡ to a northern foe
　Was never taught to yield:

---

* The English Army, on the 16th, "the day preceding the battle," was encamped in Auckland Park.

† We are informed by a talented biographer—Robt. Harrison, Esq.,—that the Percies were descended from chieftains who aided Rolla to conquer Normandy. The Barons of Percy were nobles of repute, for nearly two centuries previous to the conquest of England.

‡ John Copeland, or John de Copeland, a Northumbrian Esquire, who immortalised himself in this battle by capturing the King, though not before David, with his laced gauntlet, knocked two of his assailant's teeth out. There are descendants of this valorous Esquire now living in the vicinity of Shotley Bridge.

Rokeby, Baliol's hearts, I ween,
  Ne'er throbbed with aught of fear,
But England's Crown, their native land,
  And Freedom, hold they dear.

The morn of an eventful day
  At length has fairly dawned,
And front to front, in glancing pride,
  The hostile armies stand.
The Prior and devoted train*
  Kneel in yon hallowed bower,
Thy holy corporax cloth on high,
St. Cuthbert, greets the azure sky,
  A solemn prayer they pour;
The hearts on yon Cathedral Tower,
  Sweet, fervent strains distil,
Which, as the liquid speech of woe,
Fall on the glittering stream below,
  And float from hill to hill
Like spirits from some hidden world
  Of pain, and love, and prayer,
They wail, rejoice, and summon aid,
In lull and swell by the breezes made,
  They glide on the pregnant air.

But hark! he trumpet sounds the charge,
  The dauntless Scots advance,
O'er haughty brows the banners wave,
  The restless chargers prance.
The English archers pour a cloud
  Of arrows through the sky,
And many a noble form is laid
  In gore to writhe and die.

---

* On the spot where "Neville's Cross" was erected in commemoration of this victory, previous to, and during the progress of the battle, and within sight of both armies, "the prior with his attendants knelt around the holy corporax cloth of St. Cuthbert, which, in obedience to a miraculous vision, was elevated on the point of a spear, whilst the remaining brethren of the convent poured forth their hymns from the highest tower of the Cathedral."

L

See, like a meteor, through the heavens,
　Intrepid Graham* is borne ;
The archers from his vengeful sword
　In nerveless horror turn :
Bravely alone he wins his way—
　A god no more had done—
Till he in the unequal fight
Falls like an eagle struck in flight,
　When soaring to the sun.
Now wounded, feeble from the fray,
　He seeks his ranks again,
With ebbing life and aspect pale,
　Mingled of wrath and pain.
Now Scotland's Steward cleaves his way
　With battle-axe and blade—
The archers waver at the stroke—
Immortal Percy's ranks are broke—
　Disordered—not dismayed.
Courage ! Baliol's horsemen come,
　With vengeance in their train :
Oh Scotia ! vain's thy valour here—
　They sweep thee from the plain !

With that unconquerable will,
　Which death may tame alone,
Impetuous David struggles still
With Neville on yon crimsoned hill,
Where life is gushing like a rill,
　And dying warriors groan.
Again brave Baliol seeks the foe,
　Resistless as a wave,
The royal guard this luckless hour
Recoil before the conquering power,
　Or die as die the brave !

* John Graham, after being refused by the King an hundred lances to
break the archers, "actuated by courage and indignation, threw himself
alone upon the archers, and dispersed them on every side, and fought
until his horse was struck by a broad arrow, and himself wounded and
bleeding, was scarcely able to regain the ranks of his countrymen with
life."

Brave Murray and his hapless few,
   Where Death and Havock reign,
By countless foes environed fight,
   But ne'er shall fight again.
" England and Victory " shake the field,
   And Scotland drinks the sound,
But "mid confusion, panic, flight,
And voices of despair, delight,
   The mingling words are drowned.

But Caledonia in the shock
   Has not forgot her King,*
The best of Albyn's sons, endowed
With courage high and spirits proud
(As light may fringe the darkest cloud)
   Around him form a ring !
But bootless all : the halo bright
Is but a ray of transient light.
     See daring Copeland spring,
Like preying tiger fiercely eyed,
And dash the glittering swords aside,
   And seize the struggling king !
Now Royal rage is worse than vain,
The monarch is a captive ta'en.

Silence again her reign assumes,
   Save on the stilly air
Falls, like a voice from out the grave,
   Some wounded soldier's prayer.
The monks have ceased their hymning strain,
   The blushing Wear rolls on,
The heart's blood of ten thousand glides
All passionless within his tides,—
   The battle's lost and won !

* " Has not forgot her King," alluding to the gallant band of Scotch
nobles, who formed themselves around their King, and fought so well,
but vainly, to save him from being taken captive by the English.

Lines on the Death of the Author's Mother, March, 1873.

'TWAS sad to part in our earthly home,
And lay thee to sleep in the grassy tomb;
To see the radiance fade and die,
And darkness steal o'er thy loving eye;
To think that Silence his seal had set
On thy heart and pale lip quivering yet;
To know that thy voice, so soft and sweet,
Which taught me infant prayers t' repeat,
For e'er was hushed to an earthly ear,
And only heard in a higher sphere.

O! sweet be thy joy on that hallowed shore,
Where thy soul finds peace for evermore
In elysian fields, where spirits dwell,
Bound in the power of a mighty spell
Thrown from the eye of Eternal Love,
Which kindles to splendour the realms above.

O! here, as free as a summer bird,
Thou'lt sing the songs that earth never heard,
Save dying ears when the angels came
The fair and loved of heaven to claim,
To bear them on wings of Love away
Through the star-gemmed blue to celestial day.

O! Tell Me Not.

 TELL me not of pleasures past,
   'Tis but an idle dream,
A ray from joyous memories cast
   On life's dark rolling stream.

For when 'tis gone a denser gloom
   Creeps o'er the troubled heart,
As shadows darkle o'er the tomb,
   And sorrow's self impart.

Like waveless ocean, dark and deep,
   Let parted moments be,
Where tamed and tired tempests sleep,
   From wreck and riot free.

And show me, as with Faith's clear eye,
   Where future glories shine,
And Virtue's immortality
   With Joy and Triumph twine.

‍hamsterley.*

Lines Written on a Visit to ‍hamsterley, November, 1883.

HOW pleasant on this genial Autumn day,
(Though blooming flowers strew not my
winding way,
And every gentle breath of western breeze
Shakes the sear'd foliage from majestic trees,
Though the bright rill is singing in mine ear
A mournful requiem over Summer's bier,
Though birds are mute, and mother Nature now
Is shining not upon the rose's brow),
To rove these solemn shades, in thought profound,
Where every spot I tread is hallowed ground.

Yet sweeter still, methinks, 'neath Springtime's sky,
To linger here would be to poet's eye,
When Nature throws her ever comely dress
Upon the grove, the field, the precipice,
And larks on rapture's wings ascend on high,
Pouring celestial drops of melody;
And the sweet thrush and blackbird cheer the day,
Or sing the quiet hours of eve away;
And every linnet's simple song is dear
As sighing zeyhyrs to the list'ning ear;
When starry flowers appear so bright they give
The soul a radiant hope, and bid it live.

* Hamsterley, on the Derwent, the residence of the Misses Surtees.

But dearer still than even these to me,
Yea, e'en the streamlet's liquid lullaby,
To stand in serious mood and muse awhile,
In pleasure lost, on this romantic pile,*
And hear, as thoughtful Surtees oft was wont,
The dashing waterfall of rocky Pont ;
Or view the tow'ring Pontopike afar,
'Neath Summer's kindly beam, or Winter's war ;
Or nearer gaze, with rapture-kindling eye,
Upon these fairer scenes of beauty by,
Where Nature's lavished smile and Art have given
A paradise to earth—a dream of Heaven.
Here classic Swinburne's† skilful hand is seen,
For yet his touches linger on the scene,
To charm the mind of taste, and lure the eye,
And breathe the author's immortality.
No wonder, then, that he whose feet have trod
These loved and dear retreats, ere yet to God
His spirit winged her everlasting flight,
  Should wish again to visit parent earth,
And roam these cherished bowers‡ of love and light,
  Which gave his soul enchantment in their birth.

---

* Handley Cross Bridge, a beautiful battlemented structure, built by the late Mr. R. S. Surtees, from which can be distinctly heard the dashing of the bold and rocky waterfall of the Pont, and seen the northern slopes of the towering Pontop Pike; and in the immediate vicinity, scenery of the most exquisite character.

† Mr. Henry Swinburne, author of "Travels in Spain," and "Letters from the Courts of Paris and Naples," a former owner of Hamsterley, whose grounds, in his hands, "soon became remarkable for being the most picturesque and well laid out of any in that part of the county; as they combined the classic precision of the Italian style, with the more wild and sylvan boldness of the English park scenery."

‡ Mr. Swinburne, who was passionately attached to the secluded beauties of Hamsterley, concludes a letter written in Trinidad, where he had accepted office, and shortly afterwards died, in 1803, with the mournful words—" Nothing interests me now : nothing but thoughts of distant home occupy my mind. I shall soon be like what we read of the Indians and Africans, that think when they die they shall be transplanted back to their native groves. I wish I could think so."

Handley Cross Bridge.

Another Surtees* eke has left his share
Of taste and beauty on these landscapes fair :
Not Surtees,† he whose genius caught its hues
Or striking colours from the Laughing Muse ;
Yet true was he to Nature as to Art,
And many a wond'rous welcome lesson taught,
And deeply 'graved them on the human heart.
And though the verdant, beauteous grove may fade,
The birch decay, and vanish from the glade,
And though the oaks, whose leafy honours wave
(Their shadows trembling in their glassy grave),
Should die beneath the crumbling touch of Time,
  Or ruined fall beneath the tempest's breath,
Still shall he flourish, as in youthful prime,
  With deep-browed Swinburne, and know nought
    of death.

---

* Mr. Anthony Surtees, successor to Mr. Swinburne at Hamsterley, was a great sportsman, and a scientific and extensive planter, whose love of woodland scenery was intense, and his admiration of his predecessor's taste in the department of ornamental planting unbounded. His friend and relative, the late celebrated historian of the county, paid him no unmerited compliment in saying that Hamsterley had improved in his hands.

† Robert Smith Surtees, second son of Anthony Surtees, succeeded to the patrimonial estates in 1838. Having been born and bred within hearing of Mr. Ralph Lambton and his famous foxhounds, he commenced his career with some account of their doings, as well as of other kennels, in the old Sporting Magazine. In the year 1831, he published " The Horseman's Manual," being a treatise on soundness, the law of warranty, and generally on the laws relating to horses. This work was written whilst the author was at Lincoln's Inn Fields, and in it are revealed his tastes as a sportsman, and his education as a lawyer. It is the more interesting because of its dedication to a gentleman whose name is a household word in the north—the late Ralph John Lambton, Esq., of Merton House, Durham. Between these two gentlemen a most intimate acquaintance existed during their lifetimes, not only as kindred sportsmen, but as personal friends. A portrait, painted by Mr. Francis Grant, was publicly presented to Mr. Lambton in 1837, and the sketch from which it was made was given to Mr. Surtees, who was mainly instrumental in the picture being painted. This sketch, which is a striking likeness of the gallant old foxhunter, occupies a prominent place above the carved stone mantlepiece in the dining room at Hamsterley. Very shortly after the publication of his treatise on the horse, Mr. Surtees, in conjunction with Mr. Rudolph Akerman, started 'the " New Sporting Magazine,"

But let me further rove, in pleasing dream,
The mazes of this pure and limpid stream,
For here are treasures still to be explored,
And latent beauties yet to be adored,—
Gardens where blushing roses erst did bloom,
And left the ling'ring breath of their perfume.
Behold Mazzunti's* walk, in soothing shade,
As 'twere for timid lovers' courtship made :
Here Swinburne often came, and left a spell
Of ghost-like presence by a lucid well,
Where oft, perchance, he quaffed the sparkling wave—
Dear Nature's nectar, or did hither lave
His fevered brow, ere yet he raised his eye
To catch the lustre of the sunny sky ;
Or feed his polished mind on features near,
So dear to him, for his sake also dear
To many others, in whose minds shall dwell
His hallowed memory and crystal well.

Still further let me trace this shadowy vale,
Whose woody depths scarce know the northern gale,

---

which he edited until 1836. "Nothing," says the writer of a memoir of
Mr. Surtees which appears in his work, "Jorrocks' Jaunts and Jollities,"
" could well exceed the success of this work. Nimrod almost immediately joined it, while Mr. Surtees himself touched on a vein of rich
humour, of which, in such a field, there had hitherto been no suspicion.
But Mr. Surtees was something more than a satirist or a humourist—he
was a sportsman, and hence the force and effect he was enabled to give
to his sketches—the foundation of truth upon which he laid his quaint,
fanciful structures." Mr. Surtees' time was, as may be well imagined,
fully occupied upon his literary labours, or in attending to the duties
that devolved upon him as a country gentleman, and a magistrate for
the counties of Durham and Northumberland. He took the deepest
interest in agriculture, and frequently presided at the annual meetings
of the members of the old Derwent and Shotley Bridge Agricultural
Society, his speeches on these occasions being redolent with wit and
humour.—*Abridged from the History of West Durham.*

* " Mazzunti's Walk," so called by Mr. Swinburne, stretching from
the east side of the Hall, skirting a dean, to a well, over which Mr.
Swinburne had placed a Latin inscription, of which he gives us, in one
of his books, an English translation, which discloses the refined taste
and poetic inspiration of the author.

And tread the pathway where a lady* roved,
A fair retreat her bosom ever loved:
A shade from noon-day heat, a shelter when
The ruthless storm-king howled across the plain.
No longer here her willing feet may rove:
On higher shores, the gift of heavenly love,
Her spirit dwelleth, where eternal rest
And rapture linger ever with the blest.
Sweet is her memory still: the needy poor
   Had cause to ever bless her bounteous hand,
And weep the heart that can relieve no more,
   Whilst wand'ring friendless thro' their native land.

Lo! the fair mansion, let me look on thee,
Thou home of Thought and Hospitality!
And with the rev'rence due the minds of yore,
Which pour rich tributes o'er the land no more,
Recall their lettered pages, and employ
My humble mind on thoughts which gave them joy;
Range o'er their fields of Fancy, and awake
Their own creations for their authors' sake:
Admire, at least, what Genius has given
(The painter's art, a glowing gift from heaven),
And every inspiration they impart
Treasure within my poor, but grateful heart!

---

  * To the west of the mansion, a secluded footpath, taking the course
of a small brook, leads the visitor for a considerable distance through
most exquisite woodland scenery. This walk was made for Mrs. Surtees,
who loved to wander here and spend a quiet hour admiring the beauties
of Nature. Mrs. Surtees, who was much and deservedly beloved, particularly by the poor around her, to whom she was ever thoughtful and
kind, died in 1879.

Temperance Poems.

The Little Bow of Blue.

HO! maiden, listen while I tell
 A story of a *bow*,
But not of such an one, I ween,
 As you are wont to know;
Though, sooth to say, it yet may prove
 As honest and as true,
As any in the land have done,
 This little bow of blue.

And, youngster, with the radiant eye,
 Proud brow, erect, and fair,
I'll tell you how you may escape
 The cank'ring tooth of Care;
And some braw lassie's azure orbs
 (Love's lightning flashing through)
May see, and prize the wearer of
 The little bow of blue.

When Winter's storms blow loud and high,
 The skies are foul with rain,
Or hailstones patter on your door,
 And smite the window pane,
And not a fissure in the clouds
 To show the heaven's hue,
I'll tell you where you e'er may find
 A tiny strip of blue.

O! blue, thou hast a magic sound,
  Whate'er thy shade may be;
Thou rob'st the skies in loveliness,
  . And tint'st the tossing sea.
The harebell by the daisied mead,
  Is beautiful to view;
But most we dote upon thee
  In the pretty bow of blue.

Yes! *bow* of chaste cerulean,
  There's something in thy name,
Breathing on Virtue's smouldering fire,
  Which kindles it to flame:
That flame flows round the hardest heart,
  And softens it like dew,
To take impressions fresh from God,
  O glorious bow of blue!

Thou hast a meaning deeply set,
  And tell'st of future joys,—
Of Pleasure's glow on earth below,
  Re-union in the skies.
'Tis sweet to dream of meeting those
  We loved,—though lost to view,—
Who may have won their victory
  By the hallowed bow of blue.

Now, friends, if Sorrow's shadows fall
  Across your brow and floor,
And Dissipation's hand has barr'd
  The blessings from your door,
I'll show you how to ope the gate
  To happiness anew,—
By taking from a christian hand
  A precious bow of blue.

The scribes are at the table,
  To take down all your names,
And tell you, through their looks of love,
  That Christ His own reclaims ;
And ladies fair with gentle hands
  To minister to you,
And give you, with their blessing,
  The happy bow of blue.

Trust not until to-morrow—
  To-morrow may not come,
And Death may intercept you, ·
  Ere you reach your wonted home.
So come and take the Pledge at once,
  A treasure tried and true,
And you'll bless the happy time you donned
  The bonnie bow of blue.

———o———

Tom Jones.

OU may talk about the joy,
  And the bliss without alloy,
  All the Bacchanalian fancies,
    And his wit—Tom Jones ;
Of the jolly-going song,
And chorus loud and long,
When merry folks among,
    As you like—Tom Jones.

You may drown your grief-worn soul
Within the sparkling bowl,
Nor reflect upon the goal
    As you're wont—Tom Jones ;
And point some rosy face
As a model of his race,
And attribute Beauty's grace
    To the drink—Tom Jones.

You may mark some haggard form,
As a prey to the reform
Touching alcoholic liquors
   Doing harm—Tom Jones;
And laugh at honest men,
Who do the best they can
To urge some temperance plan
   For your good—Tom Jones.

You may revel, you may rant,
And charge us all with cant;
Such stuff we do not want
   From your lips—Tom Jones.
'Tis the thought of better souls
Than Alcohol enthrals,
Which the brave and noble sigh for
   And possess—Tom Jones.

But your joy to grief will turn,
And, alas! such bliss you'll mourn,
And all your glowing fancies
   Turn to woe—Tom Jones.
And the revel and the song
To sorrow change ere long,
As all things really wrong
   Ever must—Tom Jones.

Though the sorrow of the soul
You may drown within the bowl,
When you look upon the goal
   In calmer thought—Tom Jones,
And the rosy face decayed
In the mould is lowly laid,
Your folly you'll upbraid,
   I've no doubt—Tom Jones.

And the form on which your eyes
Did fall but to despise,
May still have got the action
 To do good—Tom Jones.
And the honest men may still
Be labouring with a will,
To check the poisoned rill
Which has slain as many millions
 As old Time—Tom Jones.

For the cant—well, let that go:
We admit we are not slow
To strike with language stirring
 On the point—Tom Jones;
And bare Corruption's heart,
As the brave and honest ought,
Though we're bullied for the part
 Which we act—Tom Jones.

There are moments in our souls,
When the voice of Conscience calls,
Like a troubled ocean rolling,
 And we feel—Tom Jones,
That the basest passions fly,
When we dream that we must die,
And the lingering virtues sigh
 O'er the past—Tom Jones.

So remember all thy grief,
And the oft-sighed-for relief,
'Twere sweet, however brief,
 To thy heart—Tom Jones,
From hell's consuming flame,
The thirst we need not name,
That brought thee to the shame
 Which thou know'st—Tom Jones.

May thy brain (perhaps it shall)
Throw off the tyrant's thrall,
And the wormwood and the gall
   Of remorse—Tom Jones.
Then thy mind may speak the thought
Of calmness as it ought,
For a cause by virtue taught,
   Which shall live—Tom Jones.

———o———

Evangeline.

EVANGELINE! Evangeline!
   How pale, how sad thou art!
Thine eyes have lost their laughing light,
   And sorrow palls thy heart!
No more the sunny smiles of joy
   Do lighten o'er thy face;
Thy form no longer throws around
   The magic of its grace.
Thy cheek, where beauty beamed, I ween,
   Hath lost its roseate hue,
And all that made thee beauty's queen
   Hath fled for evermore.

Evangeline! Evangeline!
   Reflection well may mourn
Our happy youth and innocence—
   Which never can return.
The flowers we loved have lost their charms,
   And love is almost fled,
For what to mortal eye is fair
   When virtue's self is dead?
It makes me weep the change to dream,
   For memory drives me wild;
The surging waves of passion's stream
   Have all my soul defiled.

Evangeline ! Evangeline !
　Thy silence rends my breast ;
Thou dost not murmur, though thou hast
　No hope of earthly rest.
Alas ! I never felt till now
　Th' impenetrable gloom
Which sin hath cast around me,
　Like the shadows of the tomb.
Thou dost not murmur, though thou know'st
　Thy earthly bark is driven,
A tempest tost and shattered wreck,
　From love, and hope, and heaven.

Evangeline ! Evangeline !
　O ! wilt thou yet forgive
" The plighted husband of thy youth ?"
　And bid my soul revive
The dream of bliss thou erst inspired
　In days so long ago,
Which, like a marsh-lamp through the gloom,
　Is fading faint and low
Within my breast, whose sable shades
　Have quenched the light it knew,
When virtue smiled ere sorrow frowned,
　And I to thee was true.

Evangeline ! Evangeline !
　The children of our love
Have died ere yet their childhood fled,
　And rove in realms above :
They were not fed and clothed as ought
　A christian child to be,
And this one thought my soul enthrals
　And will not set me free.
O ! that some Lethe's wave would rise
　And sweep it from my breast,
And my sad heart be passionless,
　Or know its former rest !

Evangeline! Evangeline!
  If grief hath hallowing power,
Repentance lead the soul to heaven,
  I'm saved this very hour.
So throw the sorrow from thee, love,
  There's hope beyond the grave,
The God who spared me through my crime
  Hath yet the power to save :
And I thine evening's calm will light
  With love which yet doth burn—
A burnished sky o'er the setting sun
  Tells of refulgent morn.

Sit Down a Wee.

SIT down a wee—sit down, guid wife ;
  What ca's the tear-drap to your ee?
O! weel I ken o' inward strife,
  That tears thy tender breast for me.
I've seen it lang, I've suffered sair,
  And shed a thousand blindin' tears ;
But I'm resolved to sin na mair,
  And bury a' those rolling years,
If mem'ry wi' her hauntin' mirror
Does na reflect our former sorrow.

Sit down, and put your hand in mine ;
  Our better days are a' to come.
Jeanie, when first my saul was thine,
  I dreamed o' nought but love and home :
I thought that sin could hae na power,
  Nor care wi' ought o' Jeanie dwell,
But vain the vision o' that hour,
  My crimes hae made an earthly hell,
And hell itself could na reveal
A horror worse than that I feel !

And though 'tis twenty years sinsyne,
   I yet can see in thy sweet face
The glowing virtues half divine,
   And feel the magic o' thy grace ;
The thought o't warms my haggard clay,
   As spring-time's sun fa's on the earth,
The beamy splendour o' whose ray
   Ca's mony a flowery gem to birth ;
But I will mak' my story brief,
'T may waukin hope or heighten grief.

My pleasure was a' love could gie,
   When first I wandered by thy side ;
I had a' warlds could gie to me—
   My tender Jean—my bonnie bride,
But comrades woo'd me frae thy breast,
   To bouse till mornin' lit the sky ;
Fu' weel I ken'd 'twad break thy rest,
   And fill wi' scaudin' tear thy eye :
I suffered aft and sair, I ween,
To murder thus my darling Jean.

Yet on I went my devious road,
   By passion's powerfu' vengeance driven,
Like streams whase banks are overflowed,
   When thunder rains fa' down frae heaven.
The bairnies cam'—the gifts o' grace,
 Wha should hae wiled me frae my sin,
But na the charms o' ilk sweet face,
   My saul frae darkling crime could win,
And Jeanie, I beheld the while
Thy fading cheek and waning smile.

I saw the fire that lit thine eyes
   Grow dim beneath the weight o' woe,
And heard impassioned grief-born sighs
   Express thy bosom's rending throe.
I marked thee turn thine eager gaze,
   Wi' aspect hopeless and forlorn,

.To catch 'yond sorrow's gloomy haze
   A wee bit glimpse o' smiling morn,
Then turn wi' anguish in thine ee
To look upon disgrace and me.

And years hae come and years hae gane,
   Cauld death has snatched our eldest born,
And ta'en her weary aching brain
   For ever frae the light o' morn ;
And Tammie, too, is by her side,
   Nor will our Willie lang be here.
O God ! that I in youth had died,
   Then thou, my grief-worn Jeanie dear,
Na aught o' waefu' want had ken'd—
Enough the hearts o' rocks to rend.

Some blessings we hae left us yet ;
   In our wee Mary's sheeny eye
The remnants o' our hopes are met,
   Which breathes some still remaining joy.
If God awhile my health will spare,
   And thou my dwelling to adorn,
His ways shall be my greatest care,
   And kneeling humbly night and morn,
His praise shall fill my gratfu' breast,
Till death has closed mine eyes in rest.

———o———

Gough's Peroration on Water Versified.

THIS is the liquor our Father brews
   For His children here which their strength
      renews,
   Not o'er smoky fires in the simmering still
Whose choking, poisonous, gases fill
The air around with their sickening scent,
With odours of rank corruption blent,
Does our Heavenly Father in Heaven prepare

This essence of life, this water rare,
But in the green glade and grassy dell,
Where the red deer roves 'neath Freedom's spell,
And the children smile in their wonted play
When they seek the shade from the summer's ray,
There God brews it ; and down, low down
In the valley's depths where the fountain flings
To the balmy gale its liquid tune
· And the tinkling rill as in gladness sings ;
And on the mountain's towering height
Where the golden granite shines afar
Beneath the sun's refulgent light,
Where the storm-clouds brood and hold their war,
Where the thunders crash tremendously,
And away far out on the wide, wild sea,
Where the hurricane howls its music drear,
And the big waves roar the chorus here,
Sweeping the march of Our Heavenly King.
There He brews it—this soul of life—
This water pure of health so rife, ·
And everywhere 'tis a beauteous thing :
In the dewdrops fair as they gleaming lie
On their velvet couch in the violet's eye,
Singing so sweet in the summer rain,
As it bends the flower on its fragile stem,
And its odours spring to life again,
Shining afar in the icy gem,
Till the trees to living jewels run,
Spreading a veil o'er the setting sun,
Or a white gauze the midnight moon to pall,
Sporting in every waterfall ;
In the glacier's bosom sleeping,
In the lashing hail shower dancing,
Folding its bright snow curtains round
The wintry world in the sunbeam glancing,
Weaving the rainbow's hues profound,—
That seraph's zone of the lovely sky,
Whose warp's the gleaming raindrop of earth,
Whose woof's the sunbeam from on high
All chequer'd o'er, from their mystic birth,

With celestial flowers, by refraction given.
Still always 'tis a beauteous thing,
This water blest, this boon of Heaven:
No poison bubbles from its spring,
Nor madness, nor murder, from out its foam
Arise like fiends from their hellish home.
Its liquid glass no blood can stain,
   Nor widows nor starving orphans rave,
Nor weep hot tears in its depths in vain ;
   No drunkard's shrieking ghost from the grave
In deep despair shall his curses howl:
   Would you exchange it? speak out, my friend,
For the demon's drink—cursed Alcohol !

The Reformed Drunkard's Address to his Wife.

MY sweet, my patient Wilhomine !
   What anguish have thy blue eyes seen,
   What pent-up sorrow filled thy breast,
   When terror took the place of rest !
How oft those orbs, bedewed with tears,
Have looked for dawning light through fears !
You bore my slow decay of love,
While asking aid from realms above,
To snatch me from the sin, whose powers
Blight virtue's fairest, loveliest flowers ;
And tells of man's undying crime,
That haunts him still through every clime,
And rankles in his children's veins,
Who seldom know the sire who gave
The earthly hell, expressed in pains,
Which bear them to an early grave.
The gifts of gracious Heaven were ours,
Whose angel forms I ne'er caressed,
For I was swayed by darker powers
Than those which seek a nobler breast :
They lived in want and misery,

They died, and you with grief were wild,—
Alas! it was not so with me—
No sacred thought my soul beguiled;
I false to nature, feeling too,
But you to both and heaven were true.
And we are childless, Wilhomine!
For Death hath ta'en them one by one;
They moulder in the churchyard green,
And we are left to dwell alone.
Oh! when the past I dream and you,
My folly, madness, bid me start;
Remorse's tempest sweeps me through,
And preys upon my stricken heart.
Could scalding tears of bitter grief
To crime's afflictions bring relief,
Then might I hope for peace of mind,
To mix among and love my kind,
And make amends for influence spent
In driving others from content.
But there is something night and day
Which makes my calm of soul its prey,
And places suffering progeny,
And you, whom once I loved so well,
Before mine eyes, that I may see
What constitutes my proper hell;
For all, I've learnt, who harbour crime,
Shall have their earthly pleasure marred.
The truth's expressed by sage sublime:
Fair virtue is her own reward.
Fit sorrow mine—fit anguish this,
But you are blameless, and I feel
(While heaven's afflicting rod I kiss)
A purpose in me like the steel,
Which bends but will not break, so strong
My soul hath waxed to face the wrong.
I pledge thee in this subtle grief
Which asks, nor claims, nor seeks relief,
Remembering God beholds the vow,
Whose spirit surely fills me now,
That I the poison cup will spurn,

Nor treat its votaries hence with scorn;
For who that finds the shores of peace,
From danger's tossing ocean free,
Would not at once desire release
To erring brothers still at sea?
Tho' 'tis God's will that those who err
Must suffer conscience's keenest woe,
Remorse will seize the murderer,
Though human law the lash forego.
It is not scorn and hate they need
Who quaff the dregs of misery's bowl;
They reap in suffering for the deed,
And hasten to an awful goal,
Except unearthly hands to save
Are stretched to check the rolling wave
Of passion ere it 'whelm below,
Who else to trembling madness go.
It is thy smile, philanthrophy,
Inspired by christian charity,
To soften, soothe, make chaste the heart—
Go forth and do thy holy part.
Shame on the thoughtless government
That sees the land with darkness pent,
A licensed fountain flowing free
To quench the fire of liberty;
Which plants a fiend in many a heart,
And preys upon the nobler mind,
The soul of virtue, love, or aught
That throws a blessing o'er mankind,
But lack the courage to upbraid,
And truckle to the demon's trade,
And tremble lest, in evil hour,
The slaves of wrong should snatch their power;
But there is waking in the land
Than this an impulse more sublime,
And armèd right may yet command,
And baffle hosts that foster crime.
Then let me suffer all that's known
To those who dare to follow light,
Which flashes from the eternal throne

Like meteor's radiant fire by night,
And be a unit of the throng
Of those who bravely face the wrong ;
And if our army conquered be,
Who strike to quench a nation's woe,
Our death were immortality—
Remorse the victor should o'erthrow !

————o————

The Monarch Alcohol.

ASKED of the Monarch, called Alcohol,
If ever he blessed a single soul ;
And, alas ! he cast an answer down,
With a demon glance, and a sable frown,
Which bade my throbbing heart declare
A spirit infernal had spoken there,
For the burning speech that his lips did breathe
Was fraught with the pangs of woe and death.
I will give you all, with reflection's aid,
The burden of what the monarch said:—

I roam the earth, and I sail the sea,
I flit as on wings of the viewless wind,
I reign supreme where'er I be,
And fetter the powers of the gifted mind;
I tell my votaries that rosy wine
Will give them a joy that is half divine,
That pleasure's imparted to all who quaff
Expressed in the ring of their merry laugh.
I meet with a maiden of flowing hair,
With a breast as pure as a maid's may be,
And as free as the wand'ring desert air,
And joyous as mountain melody ;
Through society I cast her a spell
Which serves, I ween, my purpose well,
To custom a slave, she fears no blame,
And I lead her on through sin to shame.

I behold the youth with his proud bright eye,
And cherry lips that have breathed no lie;
I touch him with my magic power,
And his freedom dies from that very hour.
Now he follows me on where'er I call,
To the cottage board or the festive hall,
Where my praise he sings, and my slave shall be,
And I know to the grave he shall follow me.

To the peaceful cot, where the woodlands blow,
The home of love and truth I go,
Where virtue shines in her humble sphere,
And all is fair and lovely here;
I look on the quiet with envious eye,
And resolve that its fairest blooms shall die;
I woo the husband to join my train
At the village inn, just o'er the plain,
Where I, the soul of their social pride,
The slayer of Care, shall e'er preside;
Though I know my wizard wiles may fail,
I try again, and at length prevail:
And I wot, whoe'er my votary be,
To the silent grave he shall follow me.
When years have fled, I take a roam,
And visit again that cotter's home:
The scene is changed! for Pity tells,
With tearful eye, where Sorrow dwells.
The father has gone to his last long sleep,
The widow and children in sorrow weep;
And I laugh as I say, with fiendish pride,
" Ah! thus have virtue and quiet died!"

I visit the pompous lordling's hall,
And scatter discord over all;
From a weak, fond mother, her eldest born
Like a tempest-ravished flower is torn.
But the triumph's mine, for I deal the blow
That lays their pampered loved-one low;
And laugh again o'er my victory,
For I knew to the grave he would follow me.

I traverse the squalid haunts of men,
To muse on those who wear my chain;
And hear with delight the starving child,
With piteous cries and accents wild,
Begging a morsel of bread, that rest
May visit again his weary breast;
But the sire cares naught for his wails and cries,
Or whether he lives, or whether he dies;
For 'tis long ago since he joined my roll,
And is on his way to a drunkard's goal,—
For 'tis true, whoe'er my votary be,
To the grave—to the grave—he shall follow me.

To the fairest spots of earth I go,
And change them to scenes of sin and woe;
Though the Indian strode in his majesty,
As free as the birds of the mountains are,
I fettered his steps, and dimmed his eye,
And lessened his vigour in toil and war;
And now he is true to his cup and chain,
As any slave of my lowly train.

Thus on and on through the earth I fly,
Imparting a canker that will not die;
Till numbers on numbers have legions grown,
And army on army I count my own:
And statesmen tremble, but may not dare
To wage against me an open war;
For they know my slaves no pains shall spare
Their hopes of victory to blight and mar,—
For if once they quaff of my spirit free,
I know to the grave they shall follow me.

The monarch who rules his kingdom well
May boast the power of his magic spell.
The Emperor, too, on his throne of pride,
In splendour may roam his dominions wide.
He may mutter alone to his despot soul,
That his power extends from pole to pole;
The Sultan, the King, and the Shah may tell,

N

That their subjects flatter and serve them well :—
Their sway has its limits, but mine has none,
For I rule the cot, the hall, the throne,
The kingdom, the empire, and all I've ruled,
The wisest, the wittiest, the bravest fooled.
I'll rule the new, as I ruled the old,
Assyria, Greece, Carthage, and Rome the bold;
I saw them rise to their glory's bloom,
I saw them decay and sink to the tomb ;
And other lands I rule, called free,
Shall share in such a destiny.
Am not I the Monarch of Monarchs, then ?
The victor of victors, enslaver of men ?
The subjects of others escape their sway,
And steal to other lands away;
But whoever ! whoever ! my votaries be,
To the grave—to the grave—they shall follow me !

———o———

Strike.

STRIKE ! sufferer from the Poison Cup,
　　Remorse's pang, exhaustless Woe,
　　Strike ! and thy God will help thee up,
　　And bid thy soul with pleasure glow.
Strike for the shore where light doth shine,
　　(To save thy soul from ruin's wave),
The spark is from the fire divine
　　That haunts all mortals to the grave.

Strike ! maiden, while thy charms have power
　　Against the drink-fiend of our land,
And give thy beauty—virtue's dower—
　　To him who quaffs not—with thy hand.
Strike ! and the victory shall be thine,
　　With hallowed rights' eternal fire,
For better hadst thou lonely pine
　　Than dwell with one of low desire.

Strike ! mother for the right to keep
  Thy hearth from all pollution free,
That burning tears thou mayst not weep
  O'er sin and starving progeny ;
Strike that the altar of thy breast,
  Home sacred to thine inmost heart,
May never know that sad unrest
  With which a drunkard's dwelling's fraught.

Strike ! youngster with the radiant eye
  Undimmed by dissipation's hand,
Strike ! that the shrine of Liberty
  May flourish in thy native land :
Strike with the will that nerves the brave,
  The axe of truth thy weapon be,
And wrong shall find an early grave,
  And right shall shine for thine and thee.

Strike ! manhood for your country's sake,
  Your fathers' dust, their memories,
That you may with the just awake
  To " bloom immortal in the skies :"
Strike ! at the source of England's crime,
  Her moral's bane, her upas tree,
That man may find a fairer clime
  Wherein to flourish and be free !

Index.

Geo. Neasham, Printer and Publisher, Durham.